Becoming Love

Compliments from:

The Mulberry Books, LLC
8330 E Quincy Ave
#211 Denver, CO
80237
www.TheMulberrbyBooks.com

Becoming Love.
Copyright © 2020 by Shearon Pearson Epps.

All rights reserved. No part of this book may be reproduced in any form or by any electronic or mechanical means, including information storage and retrieval systems, without permission in writing from the publisher and author, except by reviewers, who may quote brief passages in a review.

This publication contains the opinions and ideas of its author. It is intended to provide helpful and informative material on the subjects addressed in the publication. The author and publisher specifically disclaim all responsibility for any liability, loss, or risk, personal or otherwise, which is incurred as a consequence, directly or indirectly, of the use and application of any of the contents of this book.

All scripture references are from the Authorized King James Version Bible.

ISBN-13:
978-1-952405-18-1   [Paperback Edition]
978-1-952405-17-4   [eBook Edition]

Printed and bound in The United States of America.

Published by
The Mulberry Books, LLC.
8330 E Quincy Avenue,
Denver CO 80237
themulberrybooks.com

SHEARON PEARSON EPPS

Dedication

To my siblings:

Anne, Ida, Joseph, Adam, Betty, Timothy, Mary, Martha, Larceno, Winston, Meritha, Trotzky, Travaris, Nyeasha, Camillius, Judy, Johnny, Helen.

I love you all.
Thank you for all your love and support.
Pearson Pride World Wide.

Contents

Dedication iv

Chapter 1 1
Chapter 2 11
Chapter 3 25
Chapter 4 33
Chapter 5 42
Chapter 6 55
Chapter 7 68
Chapter 8 81
Chapter 9 98
Chapter 10 108
Chapter 11 113
Chapter 12 126
Chapter 13 137
Chapter 14 145
Chapter 15 154
Chapter 16 163
Chapter 17 176

* * *

*All scripture references are from the
Authorized King James Version Bible*

Chapter 1

"Father, You are an amazing God. We thank You for the many times You have come to our rescue. You have been our Provider, our Protector, our Savior and our Friend. You have been everything we need You to be. Now Lord, we need You to be our Healer."

I place the palm of my right hand gently on Angela's jawline. I can see she is in pain. Her face, wet with tears, melts into my hand. I continue to pray.

"You created us, and You know every inch of our bodies. Something is broken in Angela and only You can fix it. The doctors are trying but they are limited to what You allow them to understand. Help them to diagnose Angela's condition so they can move closer to a remedy. We know You are in complete control. We ask You to send down Your healing touch. Whether through the doctors or Your sovereign power, we need You. Angela has endured so much with this sickness and we ask You to ease her pain. We know You don't make mistakes. Give her peace of mind as You work on her situation. Help her to trust You through this difficult time. If You brought her to it, You can bring her through it. We believe everything works for the good of them who love You. Give her a testimony to help someone else grow closer to You. We are leaning and depending on You, Jesus. Help us to trust You completely. And we will forever give You the praise and the glory. In the mighty name of Jesus, we pray. Amen."

"Amen," Angela whispers through tears. She holds me in a long embrace. "Thank you, Michelle. I couldn't ask for a better friend."

Angela Reynolds and I have been friends since grammar school. We do not have much in common, but she is what I consider my best friend. Sometimes we go several weeks without communicating, but we are always here for each other. A few months ago, Angela began having severe abdominal pains. The pains were random, sometimes several weeks apart, but when they hit, she said they were unbearable. She described it as the most agonizing pain she had ever experienced. Combined with the occasional migraines she has endured since high school; she is hard to be around sometimes.

"Anytime," I tell Angela. "You know I will always be here for you."

She releases me from the hug and wipes her tears with the bottom of her hand. "I don't know what I would do without you. I would probably be in a psych ward by now," she says with a weak smile. Angela has a way of making people feel sorry for her.

"You are going to make it through this. God has not brought you this far to leave you," I assure her. "Let's get out of here. Do you want to grab some lunch?"

"Not today," Angela replies. "This has been a rough morning and I just want to crawl back into bed. I almost stayed home from church, but I wanted to make sure you prayed for me before you went home to that demanding husband of yours. You know he wants you to come straight home after church and work."

Richard is demanding, but I do whatever is needed to keep peace in my marriage. He only wants me to come straight home after work and church so I can prepare his meals. He does not like to wait on his food. If I call and let him know where I am and who I'm with, He does not raise a big fuss. He has never had a problem with me being with Angela. We have been friends since before our marriage.

"I know, but if I call and tell him I'm with you and will cook his favorite meal when I get home, he is usually good with it," I explain to her.

Richard Moore, my husband, and Angela do not get along. He was a couple of years ahead of us in school and the captain of the football team. When I graduated from college and came back home, I ran into Richard one day at the grocery store. He approached me and looked down with that beautiful smile, and I was instantly mesmerized. Of course, Angela objected to our relationship. She said Richard had been a womanizer since high school and he would never change. Six-feet-seven, broad muscular shoulders with that hickory brown smooth skin; to me, he said all the right things, looked at me the right way and had my head in the clouds after about a month of courtship. Why she objected, I don't know, but that did not stop me from falling for him.

The church is almost empty after Sunday morning service when Angela asks me to pray for her. Pastor Marc Collins preached a great sermon, 'Real Men Serve God.' Richard should have been at church today. He could have benefited from that message.

"You should ask Pastor Collins to pray for you. You know he'll be more than happy to," I say as we walk to our cars.

"Pastor has been very supportive, but I feel better when you pray for me. It feels more personal. Besides, it's hard for me to concentrate when Pastor prays for me. That is one good looking man you know."

"Listen to you," I say smiling. "That is a married man."

Although, I must admit; Pastor Marc Collins is a very handsome preacher. He takes his devotion to God very seriously. I have seen him brush off several women as they made advances or tried to get his attention.

"I know he's married, but his wife travels all the time. He is home alone way more than any man needs to be," Angela replies making quotation marks with her fingers as she said 'travel.'

"I thought you were feeling bad. Do I need to borrow some of his prayer oil and pray for you again?" I ask jokingly.

"Maybe I should go and ask him to lay hands on me, both hands, all over," Angela said animatedly.

That made me laugh. "Girl if you don't behave yourself. I thought you were having a bad morning?"

"I am, but you know that man is fine."

"I'm a married woman," I reply.

"You're not blind though, and I'm not married so I can look," is Angela's comeback.

Even in our late thirties, Angela feels marriage is a waste of time. "Why marry one man when you can have several give you what you want," she always says.

Angela is beautiful. Five-feet-six with her light caramel complexion, jet black hair hanging to the center of her back and curves in all the right places, she attracts men like flies to a barbeque. She says you can never have too much male attention.

"God has a way of keeping us when we want to be kept," I say giving her that 'be serious' look.

"All right Mrs. Holy," Angela says. She knows how to get under my skin. "When are you going to accept your call into ministry? My aunt says she can see it all over you. She is very good at reading people that way."

I frown at the subject change. I did not want to have this conversation again. Her cousin is an associate minister at the church, and he complains of the extra time the ministers must put in, not to mention the night classes and weekend conventions they are required to attend.

Being a minister is not something I aspire to be. I believe our pastor is doing the work of God but having to put in more time at church and deal with some of the personalities is not something I care to endure. I would rather learn on my own time. I have taken several Bible classes and ministerial seminars. I'm fascinated with learning more about God and His Word. But, the idea of being surrounded by opinionated men trying to show their superior knowledge over one another is not appealing to me.

"You know how the district church leaders feel about female preachers. And besides, we have enough people and churches out there eager to tell people what God says they should do. I have no desire to join the chaos," I reply. "Besides, I'm content teaching the youth. They listen sometimes. Most importantly, God has not called me to preach and if He is listening to my prayers, that won't happen anytime soon. Now, enough about me. When is your next doctor's appointment?"

"I have an appointment with Dr. Green for more tests Thursday morning. I am so tired of being poked and prodded. I'll be so glad when they figure out what is wrong with me. This has been going on for months and they are no closer to a diagnosis. What is wrong with me?"

I can see and hear the fatigue in Angela's voice. My heart goes out to her, but I don't know what else I can say to ease her pain. We are standing at her car door. Angela leans against the car and exhales a deep breath.

"You're tired. Do you want me to drive you home?" I ask.

"No, I'm fine. I didn't sleep well last night. I'll be home in a few minutes."

"OK. Go home and get some rest and I will check on you later," I instruct her.

With another hug, we both get into our cars and drive off.

Over the years, Angela and I have developed a casual but understand friendship. Angela spends most weekends at parties or in the clubs. I gave my life to God when I was in college and lost interest in the dismal party life I did have. I'm not the type of person to hang out with many people. Miraculously, Angela and I remained friends over the years. Most of my friends wanted nothing to do with me when I began talking about Jesus and His goodness.

She listens to me vent about my marriage and we discuss happenings in the church. As long as I do not get too deep into talking about God or the love of Jesus, she is content talking with me. It is nice to occasionally have someone to talk to. Richard, my husband, and I never talked about anything substantial. I listen to her escapades with parties, men and her dislike of her sister, Renae. She thinks Renae is prettier and often complains of the attention she gets from men, especially men Angela has an interest in. I think Renae is a sweet person, but Angela says I just don't spend enough time around her.

Angela is in church most Sundays. I explained that her spiritual walk is with God, not me. I often warn her about the natural dangers of her lifestyle, like safety, abuse and STD's, but I never judge her spiritually. She has to come to God on her terms.

We have had some rough patches over the years but managed to maintain our friendship for almost twenty-five years. Angela often speaks her mind and has a way of offending most people she meets. I have learned to ignore most of her comments as her unique personality. Here lately, we seem to spend more time together, probably because of her sickness. I can't imagine what she is going through. God has a reason for everything. I pray He reveals His purpose for her situation soon so she can move on to the healing stage of her life. As for me, I know God has been working on me. I often wonder where my life is going.

* * *

I drive home reflecting on Angela's comment about my call into ministry. God knows what He is doing, and He knows I don't want to become a pulpit preacher. I shake the thought away. I arrive home around one in the afternoon. I live a little farther from the church than Angela. When I walk into the house, Richard is in his chair watching a football game. It is hard for me to get him to go to church. He says going to church is not necessary to be a Christian. He goes every couple of months. I have almost given up on trying to convince him to go. After fifteen years of marriage, I've heard every excuse in the book. He has told me several times; he was baptized when he was a young boy and he knows he is covered by the blood of Jesus.

"All that other church stuff is manmade to get money out of people," he often says. "And you need to stop giving that pastor all your money."

I argue the church is about God, not man and not the money. He stopped listening to me a long time ago if he ever did. Richard is a stubborn, selfish man. It will take God to get through to him. It is interesting how much he enjoys the lifestyle we have because of the money and managing God has blessed us with. I make three times as much money as Richard and manage the household finances. All he knows is everything works when he needs it to.

"Would you like chicken wraps for lunch?" I ask him. I was not in the mood to cook. I prepared his breakfast before I went to church as I always do, so he should not be very hungry.

"That sounds good as long as you fix something nice for dinner," he replies.

Richard likes to eat so preparing his meals keeps the peace. But, when he is in one of his moods, he looks for things, anything to complain about. I never know when his mood swings will hit so I try to keep my guard up. They seem to come more often lately. Making sure his meals are ready seems to help. It's a good thing I'm a good cook. I have all the ingredients in the refrigerator to throw wraps together quickly. He will leave as soon as he finishes eating, so I don't have to worry about him after he eats. Spending time with me is the last thing he wants to do.

Our marriage has become distant over the years. As I prepare his lunch, I convince myself to try and have another conversation with him. After about ten minutes, I take him the chicken wraps and another beer. I see the empty beer bottle sitting on the table beside him. He knows I don't like him drinking in the house, but I lost that battle long ago. I sit on the sofa across from his recliner.

"Richard, how did we get to this point?" I ask him.

"What point?" he asks frowning.

"We were happy and in love at one point," I say.

"I still am," he replies sarcastically.

My husband and I have never been what one would call best friends, but we have had our good moments. Our marriage started with us taking vacations and going out to eat. Lately, it is rare we go anywhere together. Usually, the only time we are seen in public is on his rare Sunday church visits. We have not been on vacation in ten years. Our conversations are generally very short and to the point. He spends more time away from home than here, especially when I'm home. I learned not to ask where he is going. Depending on his mood, sometimes he tells me, but most times he doesn't. I don't know if he is cheating, hanging out with friends, working on another of his automotive projects or whatever else he could come up with. The only thing for certain is, whatever he's doing, he does not want to do it with me. I have grown accustomed to our routine. If we are not in the same room, I don't have to worry about his mood swings. Dealing with my hormonal shifts is bad enough. I'm a middle-aged woman. My emotions are all over the place most of the time.

I sat silently on the couch looking at him.

"What is wrong now woman," he grunts as he bites his chicken wrap.

"At one point, we were happy, what happened?"

"Nothing happened, I'm good with things the way they are. Stop looking for things to complain about" he snaps at me.

At home, he barely speaks to me. Our bedroom time is very sporadic and mostly about him. He has not touched me in almost three months. I am to the point where most of the time I wish he wouldn't. He made it clear several years ago, that we would only be together when he wanted to be. As his wife, I feel it is my duty to be there when he wants, so I always comply. How I feel does not seem to matter to him, until he wants something, usually money.

"We never talk or spend any time together," my voice is almost a whisper.

"We're talking now," he says never taking his eyes from the television.

"You know what I mean. As soon as you finish eating, you'll head to Paul's house, or somewhere. You always have somewhere to go, and I'm never invited."

Paul Davis is his first cousin. He runs an auto repair shop from his garage. This is what Richard considers his second home.

"You can come over to Paul's and hang out with us if you like. We'll be drinking beer and talking smack," he says with a sarcastic smile.

I can feel myself getting angry. I do not want to fight with Richard.

"I don't want to hang out with Paul and your friends. I want to spend time with my husband." My voice raises slightly.

"Well, you know where I'll be," he says and stares at me.

I stare back for a few seconds. He knows I will not come to Paul's. The atmosphere and language used there is not conducive to a regular woman and especially not a Christian woman.

"Fine." I walk to my room and slam the door.

Richard and I share a bedroom, but my room is what I considered my personal space. Richard never comes in here. He has his room he calls his 'Man Cave.' I only go in there to clean it but, I must let him know when it's scheduled for cleaning. Richard and I have no children so we both took a spare bedroom as our personal space.

I hear him when he turns the television off and opens the front door.

"Be back later," he yells as he goes out the door.

At least he said something this time.

Chapter 2

The house is quiet. I turn on some music just to kill the silence. The air feels thick. Anguish is building and I don't know if I can continue to live like this. Maybe I have waited too late. Maybe I kept silent too long. Is there anything I can do now? Usually, I am happy to have him leave. It means no arguing. He used to come up with a reason to fight just to have an excuse to leave. Now he just leaves.

I sit at my dresser looking at the mirror in from of me. Mrs. Michelle Moore. Am I still in love or just in love with the idea of being Mrs. Richard Moore? My marriage is broken, and I have no idea how to fix it. I have prayed. I continue to pray. Nothing works. I suggested marriage counseling, but Richard says there is nothing wrong with our marriage. As long as I continue to pay three-fourths the bills, prepare all his meals and allow him to come and go as he pleases, he has no reason to want to change. Why am I so unhappy? Something has to change. I feel like a prisoner in my marriage. Locked in a daily cycle I can't escape. This is no marriage. Definitely not the marriage we started out with.

Richard approached me in the grocery store five months after I accepted a position at Harthwell Consumers Inc. I was fresh out of college. It was not my plan to move back to Crossbow Virginia after school, but they offered me a nice salary and a sign-on bonus making it hard to refuse. They have some slogan about keeping local talent local and I fell for it.

Richard was sweet, charming and persistent. I could not understand why he was after me. He looked like he could have pursued a modeling career and there I was just plain. Most days I didn't even wear makeup. He insisted there was no one around to hold his interest and I was just what he had been waiting for. He proposed to me two months after we started dating and we were married a month later.

Our marriage was great at first. He blew my mind in ways I could not have imagined. Richard was the dream husband. Gorgeous and charming. I knew most of the women in town my age wanted him. He convinced me I was the only one for him. It was hard to believe. I was not flashy, exciting or outgoing. He said I was just the kind of woman he wanted. One who loves God, settled and knew what she wanted out of life; and doing something to get it. He has always been quite the charmer. He said all the women around town were boring and going nowhere in life. Of course, I believed every word he said.

I walk to the light burgundy daybed in my room and sit down. It has six matching pillows and a plush comforter folded on the arm. Richard hates the pillows on our bed, so I kept extra in my room. I hug one of the pillows and lay back on the bed.

God knows I'm not happy, but what can I do? I can't make Richard love me anymore if he ever did. Maybe this is his idea of love. He loves what I can do for him. I don't even know what happened to pull us apart. I asked him if there was someone else and of course, he says no. To everyone else, it appears we have the perfect marriage. When we are in public, he holds my hand, looks down and smiles at me. He even pretends to hold a meaningful conversation when he sees someone we know. When he does come to church, he sits next to me and throws his arm over the seat around me. He is always attentive as if he is hanging on to every word the pastor says.

Then when we are alone, all that goes away. He acts as if I'm his maid instead of his wife. God cannot intend for marriage to be this way. The Bible does not specifically say love is a requirement for marriage, but if we love Him as He commands, that love should flow over to those around us. The only time Richard mentions love to me is when he wants something and doesn't have the money he needs to get.

Richard and I professed Christianity when we married. That was one of the things that attracted me to him. I was newly saved and determined to live faithful to God. Fresh out of college with what I thought was the perfect job. Life was grand. Then here comes this tall, dark and handsome specimen showering me with compliments. Jackpot. Richard treated me like a queen. Most guys I had dated before were after only one thing. So, his interest in me as a person was fascinating to me. Since I would not sleep with him before marriage, he proposed after only two months of dating. I was ecstatic. Mrs. Michelle Francesca Hill Moore.

* * *

I never felt I had the body or looks to draw attention from boys. I came through grade school very insecure about my looks. While the other girls discussed makeup and nails, I would rather wear sweats and read a book. I did not have the figure of my friend Angela. By my sophomore year, I was five-feet-four, one hundred and fifty-seven pounds, no makeup and I dressed like a boy most of the time. I only later in life learned that Angela began to hang out with me because it made her feel better about herself. It did not matter to me. If she wanted to be my friend, I was OK with that. I was not asked on many dates, even though Angela tried to set me up on double dates with her a couple of times. They never worked. The only time boys approached me was to ask me to talk to Angela for them.

In college, when I gave my life to Christ, I had no idea how things would turn out for me. I was approached my Sophomore year by a soft-spoken middle-aged woman who turned out to be the school's choir director. After introducing herself and exchanging pleasantries, she asked me if I could sing. I told her no; I was not brought up in church and did not know any church songs. She seemed excited to hear that.

"You are just the type of person God is looking for," she told me. Mrs. Marina Cooper had a way of making me feel good about myself.

Mrs. Cooper saw through my insecurities instantly. She saw my heart and somehow reached in and touched it. I loved being in the choir. I really could not sing but that didn't stop Mrs. Cooper from working with me. She placed me with the tenors, but for a couple of songs, she had me sing bass. She said I had a female 'Barry White' voice. I didn't care. It was great to finally be a part of something encouraging.

Mr. Cooper, her husband, was the pastor of one of the local churches. The choir was often invited to programs at their church and other churches in the community. It was amazing to see adults care and put so much love and patience in the youth. They taught us to love God and to love and respect ourselves. And despite what the world taught; we should save ourselves till marriage. He often told us, "if a man or woman loves you, they will marry you instead of defile your reputation." That saying stuck with me.

One night after preaching on the love of Jesus, he explained that he could not love without first having the love of Jesus in his heart. He asked us if we wanted to be forgiven of sins and learn to love like Jesus. I was first in line. My life changed that night. Mrs. Cooper gave me my first Bible, which I still have. She told me "today is the first day of the rest of your life," and my life has never been the same.

Now, here I sit almost eighteen years later wondering what the rest of my life will hold. Will my marriage progress this way? Maybe Richard is just going through a phase in life. He is my husband and I want my marriage to work.

How can I be so depressed when I have so much more than most people? A good paying job, a beautiful home, a husband, maybe not the best husband, but he is better than many of them. I have a good church, friends and a God who loves me. Why does it feel as if something is missing?

"Snap out of it Michelle," I said aloud. "Help me, Jesus. I don't want to sound ungrateful. What is wrong with me. You have been too good to me. Help me live this life pleasing to You. Show me what it is You would have me to do."

I jump to the ringing phone.

"Hello, this is Michelle," I answer bringing me out of my silly pity party.

"Sister Moore. This is Pastor Collins," said the deep voice on the other end.

This is a surprise. Pastor Collins rarely calls me at home. Good thing Richard is not home. He already thinks I spend too much time and money at church.

"Pastor Collins, how are you? I enjoyed your sermon this morning."

"Thank you. God is good. I always feel Him working through my sermons. He always has a word for His people. How have you been Sister Moore?"

"I am good Pastor. Thank you for asking."

"Listen. I called because I need you to help me with something."

"Sure," I reply. My mind is now in full curious mode. It's not often Pastor Collins asks for assistance. I am always excited about the opportunity. Just being in his presence is enlightening. He always manages to impart wisdom into those around him. And his call could not have come at a better time. It took my thoughts away from my marriage and put them elsewhere. God is always on time.

"Sister Phillips has been struggling with an ailment for several months and called today to see if I would come to her home and pray for her. She is dealing with a very personal matter and she's not ready to share it with the church. I asked her permission to bring you seeing this is a delicate matter. She allowed me to confide in you. Can I count on your discretion?"

"Of course, Pastor. Sister Phillips is a sweetheart. I hate to see her struggling. I knew something was wrong, but I didn't want to pry."

"Meet me in her yard in an hour and I'll explain. We can go in together and pray with her," he says.

"See you then. And, thank you for entrusting me," I reply.

"No, thank you. You have more than proven your faithfulness to God and the ministry. Keep up the good work. Your service does not go unnoticed."

"Thank you, Pastor. See you in a little."

I lay the phone on my desk and look in the mirror. So many people are in much worse shape than I am. I really have nothing to complain about. All marriages go through rough patches. I will have to trust God to help mine work out for the good. I go into the bedroom to change to go to Mrs. Phillips. I pray nothing too serious is wrong with her. This will be uplifting for both of us. It always makes me feel better when I'm able to help someone else. There is so much power in our prayers.

* * *

"Moore!"

He knows I hate being called by my last name. As soon as I arrived at work, Mr. Jabbar, my boss speeds around the corner to my cubicle.

"Michelle, didn't I tell you I needed that report on my desk first thing Monday morning?"

"Qamar. I'm on it. You'll get it as soon as I'm finished." I bark back.

What a difference a day makes. If it's not Richard complaining about something, it's Qamar. Qamar ud-Din Jabbar is my boss. He is a decent manager most of the time. His broken English is hard to understand sometimes which makes communicating difficult. Originally from Palestine, he has lived in the United States for thirty years. He has worked for Harthwell Consumers Inc. for over twenty-five of those years. He is easy to work for when he is not trying to prove his superiority to other managers. He has this insecure need to demonstrate his over qualifications for his job, which usually ends with me having extra work.

"I told you Friday to make this top priority," he says still trying to be intimidating.

"You do realize I received the account twenty minutes before quitting time," I say holding my ground.

"What does that have to do with anything? If I need a report, your job is to deliver, on time," he growls raising his voice.

Without realizing, my voice goes up a notch also. "Did you forget you called me into your office last week with the overtime speech?"

"Well that was before this client came into the picture, this is important," he says softening his voice. I can see the defeat in his eyes, but he will never concede to losing a battle of words.

Settling my voice, I jump back in to seal my case. "They are all important to you, Qamar. I work hard to get everything you need, but I am only one woman. No one in the building can get you that report in that amount of time."

"My meeting is at one and I need that report before then to prepare," he says in a calmer voice.

"And you will have it, you always do," I say giving him an assured look.

I can see I have won this battle. Once he gets what he wants, he is nice for a little while.

"Now will you please go back to your office and allow me to work. I will e-mail the report as soon as it's complete."

I don't know why he panics every time we have a new product to review. We have done these hundreds of times and each time he overreacts.

He turns to walk away. I notice every pair of eyes in a ten-cubicle radius staring at us. I slide my chair to my desk and lay my head down.

"Help me, Jesus. I hope this is no indication of what my week will be like."

Being a data analyst for Harthwell's is busy work. Harthwell Consumers Inc. is a Fortune 500 company that sells over twenty-five hundred items; everything from wigs to microwaves. Working in the corporate office, my job is to analyze data from all 37 stores in the Southwest district. I receive sales reports, industry trends and consumer feedback from our stores and those of our competitors. I must organize the data by product and category, analyze it and get my manager an 'easy to read report' to present in his monthly meetings. My department focuses on larger ticket items. From my reports, they decide which items to keep on the shelves and which ones to discontinue.

My job is pretty routine until a new item comes up and Qamar goes into panic mode, which unfortunately happens at least once a month. Bringing in a new item is harder because it usually means something must be removed that it's going to replace. There is only so much space on the store shelves.

The new hot item on the market is the Rasmin Garden Robot. This robot trims grass, mulches leaves and removes snow. Designed to look like a toy truck, it will perform yard work and entertain the kids at the same time. I have three hours to deliver Mr. Jabbar a report that will determine if Harthwell will invest in the Rasmin Garden Robot or not. He could have given this account to one of the other analysts, but that's the reward I get for being good at my job. Do a good job and get more work.

I look at my watch. It's five minutes after nine. At least I was able to put my purse down this time before he charged in. I need to e-mail him the report by noon so that he will have time to review it before the meeting.

"I need coffee," I say heading to the coffee pot.

One good thing about work is, I'm usually too busy to think about how miserable my marriage is. With so much transforming and data wrangling, my mind is constantly contemplating the best output for the reports. At breaks and lunch, I mostly sit alone with my nose in a book and my earbuds in to rest my mind. Rarely do I sit with co-workers for small talk. Conversations on politics, vacations, complaining about Harthwell's policies that we can never change or why Bill is sleeping with Jane are not appealing to me. I'm not anti-social. My co-workers respect that I like to take breaks alone. I smile and greet everyone. Most people love to be noticed, so I am greeted with humor and short conversations throughout the day. We talk throughout the day, trying to decipher data that has come to us incomplete or out of order. It's just hard for me to connect with people. When profanity and gossip are their first language, it's uncomfortable trying to hold an interest in the conversation.

I finish the report for Qamar on time only to have sixteen more accounts like it waiting on my laptop. I often wonder, there must be more to life than this. I come to a job that pays good but is not fulfilling. I go home to a marriage that is not satisfying. Then I go to a church that is gratifying but routine. Is this all there is? Should I be seeking more of God or doing more to find happiness for myself? God created us and Jesus saves us, but what does all this mean? Am I where I am supposed to be at this stage in my life? What does my future hold?

* * *

"Michelle, oh Michelle, it's awful," Angela calls me Tuesday at work very upset and crying. "Dr. Green called me into his office today with test results."

I forgot to call Angela Sunday and check on her. The pastor called me to go with him to see Mrs. Phillips and I did not get around to calling her. I decided to wait until after her appointment on Thursday to check on her.

"Calm down Angela," I say softly. "What did he tell you?"

"I don't want to talk about it over the phone. Can you come over?"

"I'm at work, Angela. Can it wait until I get off work?"

Angela has never worked. She managed to get on disability after high school because of her reoccurring migraines. With all the support from her male acquaintances, she lives almost as well as I do.

"Oh Michelle, I need to talk to someone. I'm scared. You're my only true friend and I need you to pray with me. Please come over."

I exhale a deep breath. I hope Angela didn't hear my discouragement. Sometimes she overreacts. I hope this is no one of those times. "Let me tell Qamar I have to go. I'll be there soon."

"Michelle, you're the best. Thank you so much. I'll see you soon."

I have always had a soft spot for Angela. She never applied herself in school but came through with decent grades. She speaks her mind most of the time but can be very sweet when she wants to be. Angela wears her emotions on her sleeve, so whatever she is feeling, she displays with her words and actions. She is not an evil person, but you do not want to get on her bad side. With Angela, it is all about what Angela wants. Even when she does something nice for someone else, there is some benefit in it for her. She accepts me as I am, and I have no problem accepting her. We have just learned to make it work for us.

She was there when I needed a friend and I never forgot it. My sister Renaye died in a car accident when I was fourteen. We were very close. I was a year older than Renaye, but most people thought we were twins. We did everything together. I was so upset when she passed. Angela begged her parents to let me stay with her for a week. She was such a good friend. She became my sister that weekend.

We were very close after that. It was only when I went off to college that we began to drift apart. Once I returned, she preferred the clubs and I would rather be in church. A bond was formed that week and I did not want to break it, no matter how different our lives become, she is still my best friend.

I arrive at Angela's apartment around one in the afternoon. She meets me at the door with tears running down her face.

"What's wrong?" I ask as I step in to embrace her.

She cries uncontrollably.

"Come on and sit down." I walk her to the couch. "What did the doctor say?"

She pulls a rag to her face and blows her nose. Folding it, she washes the tears away. She inhales and holds it a few seconds, then exhales blowing to level her breathing.

"There are several things wrong with me," she begins.

She grabs a folder from the coffee table, opens it and hands it to me.

Pseudomyxoma peritonei (PMP).

"What is Pseu-do-my-xo-ma pe-ri-to-ne-i?" I ask slowly trying to pronounce the words.

"I don't know. I can't even pronounce it. It's some rare condition that started in my appendix and went through my stomach. Something like a jelly tumor. He said only one in a million people get it. They had to look at the X-rays from my CT scan from several different angles, putting them together to diagnose me. He had me drink some special dye to get pictures of inside my belly and other areas," she explains.

"Angela, I'm so sorry. Can it be treated?" I ask.

"I don't know. I got confused and didn't understand all they told me. They have to send it off to see if it is cancerous. Doctors don't really know what causes PMP. It doesn't run in families. They can't link it to anything in the environment. They gave me all these papers explaining my symptoms. They say it's small and they want me to come in regularly for them to check on it. If it is cancer, they handed me paperwork on the different surgeries and chemo options. Michelle, I'm scared."

I wrap my arms around Angela and pull her close to me.

"I know Angela, but you are not alone. I will continue to pray, and we can ask Pastor and the church to pray also."

"We can tell the pastor, but I don't want the church to know," Angela continues. "That's not the only thing."

"What else could be wrong?" I exclaim.

She looks at the wall and then back at me.

"I'm pregnant."

"You're what?"

"Pregnant." She never looks up at me when she says this. "I tested negative for pregnancy at first. They missed it upfront. They started looking for everything else. They said the eggs fertilized in my fallopian tube which can easily be missed. They called it an ectopic pregnancy or something like that."

"Angela, I'm so sorry." I rock her from side to side still holding her.

"They said I need immediate surgery to remove the fetus. They said my tube could rupture at any moment killing me. I convinced them to give me two days to think about it. "

"What is there to think about Angela? You could die!" I almost shout.

"There is a one to two percent chance the baby could survive. With the right treatment and monitoring, we both could survive," she explains in a pleading voice. "I know I have never mentioned it, but I really want children. I am thirty-seven years old and don't have anything to show for my life. I have been thinking about my future lately and I want more."

"But two percent, is that worth the risk. You can live and try again later."

"If this tumor turns out to be cancer, I may not get another chance," Angela says.

I can tell this is tearing her up on the inside. Having to deal with her physical complications and then have a pregnancy decision on her mind. I don't know what to tell her. I understand the desire to want kids. I want children also, but Richard does not. After many failed attempts on my part to convince him to have a baby, he finally instructed me to make sure I didn't get pregnant. Of course, complied.

"What are you going to do?" I ask.

"I don't know. I have to go back for surgery in two days, but he told me if I saw any spotting to call him immediately. Will you pray with me again? Then I want to try and get some rest. This day has worn me out."

"You know I will. Do you need anything else before I go?"

"Not right now, I just need some rest."

"OK." I place my hand on her stomach and bow my head. "Let us pray."

Chapter 3

I arrive home Wednesday evening around five-thirty. Richard is in his favorite chair, as usual, waiting for me to get home and fix supper.

"How was your day?" I ask uninterested.

I lay my purse on the table and walk into the kitchen. He does not reply. Maybe he didn't hear me, but I am not in the mood to repeat myself. I reach over and turn the stovetop and oven on. After checking the peas in the slow cooker and turning it off, I go to the refrigerator. I remove the pre-seasoned steaks and take out the meal, flour, milk and eggs for cornbread. I lean over to get the potatoes from the bottom compartment, and he walks up behind me.

"Whoa," I say as I jump and stand up. Richard wraps his arms around my waist and pulls me close to him.

"Richard, what are you doing?" I am exhausted and not in the mood for whatever he has in mind.

He pulls me away from the refrigerator and turns me to face him. The door closes. Not now. Where did this come from? He gently presses my back against the refrigerator door.

"I'm trying to cook," I protest.

He isn't listening to me. His lips come down to cover mine. Pressing me firmer to the refrigerator, his hands go everywhere. This is not his normal, casual kiss. My mind begins to work. What does he want? It has been years since Richard touched me in this way. The last time he wanted three thousand dollars for the down payment on a new truck. He promised to make the payments, so I gave him the money. I try to pull away.

"Richard," I whisper almost out of breath. I'm still trying to get away from him. Richard knows all the right places to touch. He has always known how to please me. He just chooses not to most of the time. He reaches over and turns the stove off while keeping one arm wrapped around me. I close my eyes trying to mentally fight what I am feeling. He pulls me close to him and whispers into my neck.

"Can't a man make love to his wife?"

I melt in his arms. I don't know what he wants, but I'm beyond fighting it. My head spins as my body responds to his touch. I know I am going to regret this later, but I can't resist now even if I wanted to.

* * *

I look at my watch. Ten-forty-five p.m. I must have dozed off. Turning my night light on, I look at Richard. He is still asleep. I can't help but wonder what he wants. Maybe it's tires for his truck, or money for a part to go on that antique car he claims to love working on. It can be for another of his and Paul's fishing weekends. Or, maybe he heard me this time and wants to work on our marriage. I will not even allow myself to dwell on that thought. I have tried so many times, why should this time be any different. Richard wants something. But for now, he has not gotten it.

Richard lay on his stomach with his head resting on the back of his hands. The comforter down to his lower back. He is still breathtaking to look at. Richard goes to the gym three times a week, and his body looks immaculate. It has always been hard for me to accept someone as handsome as he would be interested in me. I upgraded my wardrobe to more align with his, but he is still in a notch above most men. Someone I have always felt was out of my league. For now, this gorgeous man lay in bed beside me and he still has not gotten whatever it is he is after. Maybe I'm at an advantage for a change.

I run the tip of my fingers over the back of his hand and trace his arm to his shoulder then to the back of his neck. He still does not move. I run my fingers from his neck down the center of his back opening my hand to feel the masculinity of his muscles. His skin is smooth. When I reached the comforter, his lower back arches. He still does not awaken so I repeat the process.

This time he grunts and rolls his shoulder to remove my hand. He shifts over and looks at me with a disgruntled look. His eyes hold mine for about ten seconds and then his expression softens. He smiles. I guess this is where he realizes he has not gotten whatever it is he wants. He turns his body and pulls close to me. I can't help feeling he doesn't mean any of this. His initial reaction when he awakened confirmed my suspicions. I close my eyes to mentally control my physical reaction. He takes my hand and kisses it.

"You know, Paul finally found that transmission I need for my car," he says.

Here it comes.

"Really Richard," I say pushing away from him. "Was all this necessary."

"What are you talking about."

"If you want something, just ask. You don't have to pretend to want me just to get money out of me."

"Maybe I just wanted to be with my wife. You are the one complaining about we don't spend enough time together. I know you enjoyed it."

I roll my eyes. I did. I really did, but that is beside the point.

"It's not just about being physically satisfied, I have an emotional side too."

I know Richard hates these types of conversations, but it's hard for me to continue to keep silent. I am miserable. He lays back on the pillow. He has not gotten what he wants. I plan to use my advantage this time. He exhales.

"What do you want from me?" he asks.

"I want you to want me. All of me."

"I thought I just proved that. I can prove it again if you want."

He cups both hands behind his head and flexes his muscles. I look down his body. The comforter lays just below his navel. That sounds so tempting. I close my eyes for a second. Whew, this man looks good. For a brief second, my imagination entertains the thought of enjoying him again. Focus Michelle. If I give in now, I don't know when I'll get him to listen to me again. I look up and meet his gaze. He has that manipulative smile he has used on me so many times before.

"Richard, our marriage is broken. We don't spend any personal time together. When we are in public, you hold my hand and treat me like a queen. At home, you barely speak to me then leave me here alone. I used to think the outside attention was sweet, now it's just annoying. Why do you do that?"

"So, you don't want me holding your hand in public?" he asks.

"I want to know why you treat me differently in public."

He pauses and looks at the ceiling as if debating how to answer.

"Because you are mine," he answers.

"Huh." I reply.

"You're mine and I want all other men to know that."

I give him a puzzled look.

He continues to explain. "Men are different from women. When a woman sees a man in a happy relationship, she goes after him. Something about seeing another woman happy makes her want to break it up. Men generally stay away from women they see in happy relationships and go for the broken and depressed ones. We want to give them what they are not getting at home. I do that to keep other men from approaching you."

I look at him for a few seconds. He has a point. I had never thought of it that way. Men and women do think differently. At least he thinks someone else may want me.

"So, you want to make sure no other man gives me what you're not giving me at home," I say with a frustrating smile.

He frowns at me. "What are you talking about, woman?"

"Before now, it has been three months since you touched me," I declare.

"It has not been that long," he says. I can see he is thinking and realizes it has.

"And you don't have to worry about me. I made my vows to God long before I made them to you. My question to you is if you are not getting it from me, where are you getting it from?" I ask.

I'm feeling bold now. Richard has a very healthy appetite and he knows I am aware of it.

"I've just been busy and had things on my mind," he tries to explain.

"Things like what? You have a helpmate to help you through whatever you are dealing with. Why won't you let me help you."

"It's nothing. You wouldn't understand. Besides, you do so much around here, I would hate to burden you with my little problems."

"There you go shutting me out again. I have no idea what you deal with every day. You never talk to me. Richard, how is our marriage supposed to work if we never talk?"

I can see he is getting frustrated. He turns to roll out of bed. But it hits him that he has not fulfilled his original purpose. He lays on his back again.

"Michelle, you're my wife and I love you. What else do you need."

I look around the room. I need my partner but how do I explain it to him? Maybe he is doing the best he can with our marriage. I guess my job is to find a way to live with it. He can tell from my expression he has won this discussion. He takes my hand and kisses it. It's time for him to let me know what he really wants.

"We have been together for so long. I do love you. I know I have been busy but as soon as Paul and I get my car running, I promise, I'll spend more time with you." Richard's promises are like using a noodle strainer to hold water.

He sees the blank stare I'm giving him, but he knows what he wants, and he does not stop until he gets it. I hate he has this kind of power over me.

"We only need thirty-five hundred dollars to get the transmission. Paul and I will install it. I took Friday off. We are planning to leave Friday morning and drive to Kentucky to pick it up. It's going to take us four and a half hours to get there so we thought we would stay overnight."

The more he talks the more my stomach turns. How can I be so weak? I want my marriage to work, but there must be a limit to what I'm required to do to make it happen. Even though I don't want to, I know I am going to give him the money. I just want him to stop talking now. I can't bring myself to say anything. He becomes more animated.

"The guy that's selling us the transmission says they have some great fishing places. We are going to take our fishing gear and if they are biting, we may stay until Sunday morning. He says they bite best at night."

I roll over and sit on the edge of the bed.

"I'm going to take a shower. I'll leave a check on the dresser before I go to work," I say sounding defeated. I stand and walk towards the bathroom.

"Thanks Babe. You're the best," he yells. "Could you fix me something to eat when you come out of there. I'm starved."

I close the door behind me and sit on the toilet. The tears begin to flow. I don't want him to know how upset I am. Is this what the rest of my marriage will be like? I begin to talk to God.

"Why am I the only one putting into this marriage? We are both Your children. Your Word teaches us to love. I don't think Richard knows what love is. Our marriage should be equal. How do I continue to love someone who does not love me?"

"You love because I am Love." I hear the words in my Spirit. God seems to speak when I least expect it.

"I know, but he should love also. He says you are in him too," I protest.

"I didn't ask you to fix Richard. You are to love because I am love." I hear again.

It's hard to stay upset when God moves in my Spirit. When He speaks, I always find peace.

I want harmony back in my marriage. I seem to be the only one in distress.

Maybe I am overreacting. Maybe this is the way marriages progress, and everyone else is putting on the same show in public. I will remind Richard of his promise when he finishes his car. If he's willing to try, so am I. I wipe my tears and step in the shower.

Chapter 4

I go to work Thursday feeling void of something. Because of Richard's escapade last night, I missed Wednesday night Bible Study. It's like a mid-week spiritual boost to get me through the remainder of the week. I rarely miss Bible Study. Be hard to explain to anyone that I came home to a frisky husband. Maybe no one will ask. It was not my night with the kids so I should not have to explain.

I do have something to look forward to, a weekend free of Richard. I need to plan something instead of sitting around the house. I'll check on Angela. She mentioned getting a second opinion. She is seeing the doctor today. If all goes well with her, I'm taking a road trip somewhere. She can come with me if she feels up to it. Before college, she and I found places to go. I didn't have any money most of the time, but Angela always seemed to have enough for both of us. Now, we are lucky to have lunch every few months. It has been six months since we saw a movie together. Finding something we both like is a challenge. I'm going somewhere even if she does not want to go.

I have not taken a trip alone since I married Richard. This is much needed. I'll take a good book, get a room and find a nice restaurant. Somewhere on the lake. I may drive to the beach. That will be nice.

"Daydreaming again, Moore?" Qamar appears from nowhere standing over my desk. I didn't hear him walk up. He lay a piece of expensive-looking chocolate on my keypad. I always get chocolate when he knows he has gotten on my nerves about something.

"Thank you."

"Management was really impressed with your report," he says. "We went with the Rasmin Garden Robot. It is projected to bring in over seven million in revenue the first year alone."

"That is nice. It must be nice being a part of the decision making to bring in so much money for the company." I say trying to make small talk.

"It is when our suggestions pan out. When they don't, they are always looking for someone to blame." He looks around my cubicle. "Well keep up the good work."

He walks away. Qamar never lingers. I like that about him. Always short, sweet or not, and to the point. I have learned a lot working for him over the years.

The rest of my workday goes smoothly. My work has become so routine, I spend most of my day mentally planning my weekend. I inform Qamar that I want half the day off tomorrow. It will only take me a couple of hours to drive to Virginia Breach. I'll settle in my room and go walking around on the beach that evening. Find a nice place to eat, right there on the beach. I smile at the thought. Get up Saturday morning and visit Norfolk Botanical Garden. It has been years since I went there. Come back and do some shopping at the mall before I lay out on the beach with my book. This is going to be a great weekend. I really need this. I leave work excited about going home for a change. As soon as I get home today, I'll call Angela, make my hotel reservation and start packing.

* * *

I arrive home to a barely legible note on the refrigerator from Richard.

> *no super tonight. me and paul planning trip. be late when I get home.*

He could have just texted me. I guess he is afraid I would respond. Too much communication for him.

I don't care what Richard is planning. I have my own plans and they don't include him. He said don't cook so I didn't. I fix myself a sandwich and start my travel arrangements.

After my sandwich, I call Angela.

"Hey, how are you feeling?"

"I feel good today," Angela replies.

"What did the doctor say about your surgery? You forgot to call and update me," I tell her.

"I was going to call you later. I have bugged you enough at work and wanted to wait till you got home."

"You are not bugging me, Angela. This is serious and I want to be here for you as much as I can."

"I didn't allow them to perform the surgery. He took some more blood and told me again about the urgency of the operation to remove the fetus. I convinced him to let me get a second opinion tomorrow. He recommended a specialist in Indiana. I have to fly out in the morning. He said if the specialist agrees with him, he is prepping me for surgery Saturday. I hope this specialist gives me good news. There must be something they can do."

"Do you want me to fly there with you?" I ask.

"No, you have done enough already."

"But you don't need to go there alone," I tell her.

"I won't be alone." She pauses. "My sister is going with me."

"That's great. It's good to see you and Renae getting along."

"Yeah, I think she feels sorry for me, or maybe she wants to be the first one there if I croak over," Angela says.

"Don't say that. Renae is not that heartless."

"You don't know my sister," she says in a condemning voice.

"Well, at least she is going with you. I think more of her already," I say.

"You would think that Mrs. Goodie Two Shoes."

"Don't be mean, Angela."

Even in her condition, Angela wants to see the negative in everyone.

"I have to get packed," Angela says. "I'll call you tomorrow and let you know how things go."

"OK. Be safe. I'll keep you in my prayers."

I did not tell Angela about my trip. I didn't want her to think of me laying on the beach while she is going through her ordeal. I say a quick prayer for her to have a safe trip.

Still excited about my trip, I finish packing and go to my room to do some reading. I can't help but think of Angela and Mrs. Phillips dealing with their cancer. Both are young women. Mrs. Phillips is only in her late forties and must have both breasts removed. I silently pray for both ladies.

"Thank You, God, for my health and strength. It could be me." God has been good to me.

I go to bed early. I don't know what time Richard come in and for some reason, I didn't care. I want to work on our marriage, but I cannot do it alone. I'll see how he acts once his car is fixed and try to go from there.

I awaken an hour early. Richard is asleep beside me. I am excited so I get up and turn on the coffee maker. I do not want to wait on the automatic timer to start. After I dress and drink a cup of coffee, I still have thirty minutes before time to leave for work. I decide to go in early since I am getting off at lunch.

Fifteen minutes up the road I realize I left my phone at the coffee table where I was reading the morning news. Turn around or not. The thought runs through my head. I look at the time. I still have time to go home, get my phone and make it to without being late. I pull up to my house.

"Angela must have changed her mind about asking me to go with her," I say frowning when I see her car parked in my driveway. You can't show up at someone's house last minute and expect them to fly off. I'll have to talk to her about that. Maybe she is here for prayer or she needs something for her trip. This is a big decision for her, and she is going through a rough time. I walk up and open the door. I feel bad for my original thought.

Most likely, she just wants me to pray for her before she leaves. She should have called. And, maybe she tried but I left my phone. I walk in the door. Her purse is on the couch. There are two tickets to Indiana on the table in front of the couch. Maybe she does expect me to go. Where is she?

I hear voices coming from our bedroom. Why would she be in my bedroom? I step in to see Angela laying, shoes off in tank top and shorts, along my side of my bed. Richard steps out of the bathroom shirtless. My initial thought is 'Richard you need to put on a shirt.' Then, I look at the surprise on both of their faces and a different thought goes through my mind.

My chest tightens. I inhale and open my mouth, but nothing comes out. Richard freezes. Angela jumps up and stands on the side of the bed.

"I'm sorry Michelle," she says softly. She grabs her sweater off my nightstand and throws it over her shoulder.

I cough when I realize I am not breathing.

"You have got to be kidding me," I growl. I step towards Angela.

Richard races over and grabs me. My arms swing and I let out a yell that causes Richard to release me. I turn to face Angela. I'm not thinking straight. Richard grabs both my arms from behind and pulls me away from Angela.

"In my house, that I am paying for." Tears have formed in my eyes. "Get your hands off me, Richard."

I twist out of his hands and push him away with my fists. He barely moves backward.

"This is not what it looks like. I was just dressing so I could go with her to Indiana," he tries to explain.

"And why would you be going with her to Indiana?" I scream. "You don't even like her."

Angela steps back against the wall and looks at the floor. I step closer to Angela and Richard steps closer to me. I'm shaking all over. I cannot believe what I think is happening. My brain is trying to function over my growing anger and confusion.

"Why is Richard going with you to Indiana?" I stare at Angela when I ask.

"Because she asked me to go," Richard says. His voice is cold and dry.

"Be quiet Richard," I snap. I glare back at Angela. Richard has always been arrogant, but this is low even for him. This cannot be what I think it is.

"Why is Richard going to Indiana with you?" I say the sentence angrily and very slowly.

She never looks up at me. "Because it's his baby."

Feels like someone punches me in the chest. All the air goes out of my lungs. My knees give away and I go to the floor. I land on my hands and knees. How can this be? His baby? My mind is trying to decide which one of them to charge first. I decide on Richard. He did this to me. He claimed he never wanted kids. Take him out first and then I will deal with Angela. His baby? How does she know it's his? She has slept with every man in town.

Richard steps towards me. The look I give him stops him in his tracks. My mind tells my body to charge as hard as I can. Just attack him swinging. I make the motion to get up, but my body won't corporate. I can't get up. The rage that is going through me at this moment is something I have never felt. If I could move, I would rip his head off. I mentally prepare to attack again, but I'm frozen. Why can't I move? "Charge," I scream in agony. My body is frozen, and I can't control it.

I decide to verbally attack him. So many thoughts go through my head, but nothing will come out of my mouth. Words go through my head that I have never spoken in my life. The kind of language I have heard but did not know was inside me. I want to let it out. Unleash my pain on them both. I can't speak. I can't breathe. I feel anger. Confusion. Pain. Betrayal. Agony. Resentment. All overlapping and entangled into excruciating pain. The pain I want to channel to them.

I can't think. My face burns. My fists are balled so tight I can't feel my hands.

What do I do?

"Just leave Michelle." I hear the voice from inside me. I can't move. My breath sounds like a wheeze within me. I'm trying to breathe without crying out. "Stand up and leave," the voice says again. The tears are flowing as I straddle on my hands and knees. It hurts to breathe. I hear the voice, but my limbs will not cooperate. I want to get up, but I don't want to leave. I want to let these two have a piece of my mind. I want to start swinging and let the licks land where they will. I steady my breathing and then the rage becomes stronger.

"Leave." I hear it. I know it's God, but I don't want to listen. I still can't force my limbs to move. Then I feel the sobs chocking up inside me. I cough to stop them. I must get out of here or they are going to see me completely fall apart. Now, I'm just determined to get out before I break down.

"I'm sorry Michelle." I hear Angela whisper again. Her voice makes the anger worse. I stare at her with deadly eyes. I want to charge them both, arms swinging. I slowly stand to my feet. So much pain. So much going through my head. If I open my mouth, I don't know what will come out. I look at Richard then Angela. My face is covered with tears but burning with anger.

Angela continues to look at the floor. Richard stands with his cocky, proud stance. He will not admit he is wrong even with it staring him in the face. How could they? How could she? I prepare to charge again but my body locks.

"Why," manages to come out of my mouth. Why would they do this to me? Why can't I charge them? Why now? Why is all that manages to go through my head.

Angela never looks up.

"Now you know." Richard starts to speak, and I hold my hand up to stop him.

The flood of emotions takes over and I feel myself about to burst. I shake my head, turn and walk out.

Chapter 5

I manage to close the front door behind me before I break down. I lean forward and catch myself grabbing both knees. My head and stomach are turning. I feel as if I will throw up, but nothing comes out. The sobs come uncontrollably. How could they? Just make it to the car, Michelle. I stand enough to grab my stomach. It turns more. I will myself to make it to my car. Inside the car, the sobs come harder. I become angry. With myself. With Richard. With Angela. With God. Why me? Weakness. Helplessness. Fury. Uncontrolled fury.

Rage mounts within me. A frenzy more intense than anything I've ever felt before. My breathing is heavy. My mind spins. They need to pay for what they did to me. I keep a knife in my purse. Richard actually suggested I keep one with me when shopping alone. I should have bought that stun gun years ago when I got the knife. He said he was afraid I would use the stun gun on him. Ironic isn't it? I have the knife he gave me. I take the knife from my purse and put it in my pocket.

Then another thought hits me. Richard keeps a hunting rifle in the shed out back. I have never shot a gun before but how hard can it be. Point and pull the trigger. No judge will convict me. Self-defense. Jealous rage. Temporary insanity. I'll say I caught them in my bedroom. That is the truth. The jury will have to understand and see things my way. Go get the gun and make sure it's loaded. It can't be too hard. I have seen this stuff on television.

No more talking. Walk in, point and shoot. They deserve it for what they did to me. I yank the car door open. Both feet hit the ground. I'm angry. I'm focused. I'm determined. This is just the way it has to be. They can't treat me that way and expect to get away with it.

"Close the door Michelle." I hear the voice as clear as day. I ignore it. I have listened and been obedient all these years and look where it has gotten me. "Close the door." I hear it again. I step outside the car door and slam it.

"No." I scream. They cannot do this to me and get away with it. I stare into the heavens and a flood of emotions cover me. My knees tremble and give away. I fall on the car and catch myself. I know God is stopping me, but this is not fair. They hurt me. They are in my home. I have a right to hurt them. Tears pour out of me.

How could this happen? I spent so many years being the good wife only to have it thrown in my face. How could I be so stupid? Richard is not much of a surprise. I have long suspected him of being unfaithful. I was so afraid of losing him that I allowed him to do what he wants. But with Angela. Anybody but her. They always pretended to hate each other. I was so blind. How long has this been going on? Angela and I have been friends forever and she does this to me. And a baby. Richard said he did not want kids. The sobs come even harder. My mind is racing uncontrollably. The pain is unbearable.

I have served God faithfully for over seventeen years. I thought my life would get better over the years not worse. Why would God allow this to happen to me? My anger intensifies as the pain increases. My mind begins to focus on God. He is in control of everything.

"Your Word says you have a hedge of protection around Your children. I know I have not been perfect, but I have tried. I put You first. Why would You give him to me only to have him hurt me? You are in control of everything. Satan could only touch Job with Your permission. So, You allowed this to happen to me. Silence. I know You hear me."

I'm angry and in pain. I should lash out at someone, anyone. I'm the good guy here. Why am I the only one broken?

Satan has no power. Richard has no power. Only God has the power to make things happen. He is in control of everything. Why would God want me in this much pain? Is this what I get for faithfully serving Him?

"Please make the pain go away. I love You, Jesus. Please. I need You. This is unbearable. What did I do to deserve this? I'm sorry. I know You love me." My mind and emotions are all over the place. I don't understand. I am so confused. I know God is love but this does not feel like love. It feels like punishment. But, what did I do?

Breathe Michelle.

My tears continue as my mind tries to focus.

"Please. Please. Please. Please. Please. Please. I need You, Jesus. Please."

My sobs slow but the tears continue. I breathe in and out. What am I going to do?

"The joy of the Lord is your strength. No weapon formed against you shall prosper. Be of good courage, and he shall strengthen your heart, all ye that hope in the Lord."

I don't want scriptures now. I need Jesus to help me. I need him to fix this. The scriptures continue to come in my Spirit.

"Come unto me, all ye that labour and are heavy laden, and I will give you rest. Take my yoke upon you and learn of me; for I am meek and lowly in heart: and ye shall find rest unto your souls."

It is as if someone is standing over me reading from the Bible.

"Delight thyself also in the LORD; and he shall give thee the desires of thine heart. Cast thy burden upon the LORD, and he shall sustain thee: he shall never suffer the righteous to be moved. Weeping may endure for a night but joy cometh in the morning."

I feel a wave of peace come over me. My chest still hurts, but I can breathe. I reach in my glove compartment and pull out several napkins to clean my face. I need to get out of here. I can't go to work like this. I'll call Qamar and let him know I need the whole day off. I have half the day off already. I reach for my phone. Then it hits me, I never picked up my phone when I went into the house. I wipe away tears and look at my watch. I've been out here for about twenty minutes. I breathe in and out. I don't want to go back in there. But I need my phone. Jesus. Please. I've got to have my phone. Maybe they are still in the bedroom. I can go in, grab my phone and leave without them knowing. I push myself away from leaning against my car and walk to the front door.

Please, Jesus. Just let me get away from here. I need time to process all of this. I need time alone to pray.

I walk through the door as quietly as I can. When I step around the corner, they are standing twenty feet in front of me. My eyes lock on Angela first. She quickly looks to the floor. Then they shift to Richard. I couldn't look away. The rage returns. The thought of the gun returns. I am frozen, speechless. Neither of us speaks a word. All the previous emotions come rushing back through me. Richard is fully dressed pulling his suitcase. Angela stands beside him. She continues to look at the floor. Her mouth open. Panic is across her face. Richard takes his right arm and pulls Angela behind him. I guess he sees something in me he has never seen before. He has not seen me angry for a long time. I learned to control it. I don't think he has ever seen me like this. I know I have never felt this way before. I don't know what he expects me to do. I guess he knows even I have a breaking point.

I look at Angela and even in my pain, I almost feel sorry for her. Richard can be very controlling. I know he treated me that way because I allowed him to. The church has always taught that women should be submissive to their husbands. Richard takes that submission as a weakness. And when I stopped complaining regularly, he took me for granted. I prayed things between us would one day get better. They never did. And now, I don't know what to expect.

I can see my phone on the table directly behind them. I look down at it. I am not leaving this house without my phone. I guess Richard thinks I'm looking at Angela. He pulls her closer to him. I have an angry, defensive look on my face. I know my pain and emotions are showing all over me. I look at the suitcase and then back at him. My mind tells my body to charge them, but I can hear my Spirit saying, "peace be still."

"We're leaving," Richard says in an irritated voice.

I don't know how, but I manage to speak. I don't even know where the train of thought comes from. I am not even thinking about money.

"Is this where my money went," I say almost whispering.

Richard exhales as if he doesn't want to bother with me right now.

"Yes, as it has many times before." He stares at me and then unloads as if he had been holding his anger in for years.

"Look at you. You're weak and pathetic. You knew I didn't love you. I never loved you. You knew I had someone else. Yet you still did everything I wanted. No real woman will let a man treat her that way. Angela is tuff. She will curse me out, even slap me when I get out of line. Real women know how to keep a man."

Yes, I was pretty sure he was cheating on me. But why did it have to be her? He could have any woman he wanted, and he chose my best friend. The one person who would hurt me the most. I remember the knife in my pocket. My hand slowly slides into my pocket. My rage grows as he speaks, but my body won't move. He continues to talk and seems to get angrier as he speaks.

"I only held your hand in public cause I knew you would fall for any man who gave you some attention. I don't know why I thought that because no one wants you. I only did it to get what I wanted. Just simple. I don't see why you never put it together.

"After I didn't get a football scholarship, I knew I was stuck in this town. My coach helped me get an assistant manager position at his brother's auto parts store, but that was it for me. I was stuck in this town selling auto parts."

Richard was not academically intelligent, but he was built for sports. He counted on football getting him into college and then the NFL. I didn't know it when I married him. He harbored resentment to the town and everyone else for him not getting into college. He often complained about it during our marriage. It was his grades that kept him from getting a scholarship. Blaming everyone else made him feel better. He continues to attack me.

"Then here you come. Fresh out of college landing that big office job at the best paying company around."

He giggles sarcastically. My stomach turns as he speaks. His words paralyze me. I'm frozen in a daze to hear everything he has to say. I can't move or speak. The urge to attack is so strong but my legs are frozen. My fingers tighten around the knife in my pocket. I place my fingernail in the slot to flick it open as soon as I get it out of my pocket. If only my arm would cooperate.

I could stab them both now and get away with it. They are still in my house. He is enjoying the pain I am in. I feel the rage intensify. Then I look at Angela. She looks as broken as I am. Something softens in me. Still rage. Still pain. But something in me feels pity for her. Richard continues his insults.

"I figured, if I had to stay in this town, I might as well live the good life. You were so easy. You hung to my every word. I could tell you anything and you believed me. When I told you I love you, you were ready to give me the world. I never planned to marry you, but you held out. I had to marry you to get the full benefit. I knew once I got you in bed it was all over. You couldn't understand how someone like me could love you. Well, I didn't. All I had to do was touch you and you gave me whatever I wanted."

How can he be enjoying this? I am sick to my stomach. All the feeling has left my body. I am too weak to attack now if even if I wanted to. Attacking them will not take my pain away. It will only cause me more pain down the road. He giggles between each statement and looks at me as if I have no feelings at all. I can't stop the tears from flowing. If I open my mouth, the sobs will start again. So, I stand there, listening, trying to breathe without breaking down. Angela's expression is filled with pain as if she is hearing this for the first time also. He continues.

"And as for children, I always wanted a son. Just not with you. I knew one day I would get tired of you, and I wanted no ties to you. You were definitely not going to have a reason to put me on child support."

I can't breathe. My chest burns as if someone is grinding a bat into it. But all I can do is stand here and take his insults. My anger won't surface because of the pain overwhelming me. It takes all I have not to break down right here. I don't want to give Richard the satisfaction. He's hurting me. He knows it. My eyes can't hide the pain I'm in.

"We have a plane to catch. I'll get my things when I return. I need to go save my son." He grabs his luggage with one hand and drags Angela with his other. They walk out the door. Angela never looks up at me.

* * *

As soon as the door closes, I run to the bathroom to throw up. The sobs come back. This time they seem worse. The pain is definitely worse. How could he say those things? I gag and throw up again. I don't know how long I hang over the toilet before I sit on the floor. Leaning against the wall, I allow his words to overtake me. With my elbows on my knees and face in my hands, I let the tears flow. My sobs are loud, but I don't care. No one seems to care how I feel. I didn't know pain like this existed. How could he?

Since being married to Richard, I have tried to be a good wife, a Godly wife. He rarely had to ask for anything. I knew what he wanted and worked hard to provide. He got everything he wanted from me. I guess the occasional lovemaking was his way of saying thank you. Sorrow floods me. Rejection is my reward for being a good wife. Insults and pain for trying to live faithful, to him and to God. If he was so miserable, why didn't he just leave? How could he live with me and feel that way? I was not forcing him to stay. I guess he wanted his moment to wound me. Well, he got it. That hurt. I loved Richard when I married him. I loved him more than I did myself. And although our marriage was rocky, I still love him. What he wanted always came before what I wanted. His needs before my own. All to have it thrown back in my face. Fifteen years and for what?

How could he share his life, his home, his bed with someone he feels this way about for fifteen years? He says he's a Christian. How can God live in a heart like that? Did he mean what he said or was he just trying to hurt me? How could I have missed all the warning signs? Is love really this blind? It is one thing to think your husband is cheating. But, how do you know he hates you. Disgusted by you. This is so much to process.

I can't even begin to think about Angela. All those times she talked bad about Richard. Laughed in my face. Told me I was crazy for giving him so much when most of it was probably going to her. 'He should be paying you for being with you' was her big line. 'He's my husband,' I would say. 'I should give him what he needs.' All the money I loaned her when one of her gentleman friends did not come through and she never paid me back. But friends should not have to pay back was my rationalization.

I have known Angela for most of my life. She is selfish but not heartless. If she likes you, she'll give you the shirt off her back. If she didn't, you knew it. Did she feel the same about me as Richard? Just being my friend to get what she wanted. This is sickening to think about. Them both, and for how long?

Reflecting on memories and events over the last fifteen years, I try to develop some purpose and logic to what had just happened. I can't. Especially where Angela is concerned. It still hurts.

How could I be so stupid? I sit on the floor leaning against the wall for a long time.

I finally stop crying. I stand and look in the full-length mirror. I look awful. My face is swollen. Eyes red. I take a wet cloth and wash my face. Noticing my wedding ring, I hurt my finger yanking it off so fast. I almost flush it but the thought hit me. I paid for this and I work hard for my money. I lay it on the sink.

I look at myself from head to toe. What is so bad about me that he could not love. My weight is almost the same as college. One hundred sixty, pounds are not that big. My shape is proportionate with all my curves in the right places. My face is plain. I was never one for much makeup, but I wear a small amount to please him. All of this he knew when he married me.

I exhale. There is nothing I can do about it now. I need to call into work. I'll just text Qamar. I am in no mood to talk or try to explain. He'll take care of my time. He knows if I'm off work, I need to be. My hands shake so I can barely text.

I need to talk to someone but who. I usually talk to Angela when something bothers me. That thought sends rage through me again. She knows everything about Richard and me. Every time I gave him money. Every time we had an argument or at least when I got mad for not speaking up the way I should. Every time he made advances and whatever he wanted of me after those advances. When I needed to vent, I called Angela. Now what. That makes this so much harder. How could she? How long had she and Richard been together? She tried to convince me not to marry him, but I was in love. Were they sleeping together then? Wow. I was so blind.

I can't talk to my mother about this. She wouldn't understand. My father is an alcoholic who beat and cheat on her most of my childhood. His episodes have decreased over the years, mostly because of age, but he is still a jerk. He drinks a lot. She is just glad to have him home most of the time. She waits on him hand and foot. She never worked and told me that's the price women must pay to have a man take care of them. I'm glad that mindset didn't rub off on me.

I talk to my mother at least once a week. She was excited when I gave my life to Christ. She explained that her parents never took her to church, so she felt it was not important for her to take my sister and me. After listening to my enthusiasm about the choir and my growth through the church, she had my father take her to visit the church my Aunt Sally attends. He won't go into a church but won't allow my mother to drive there alone. In fact, she is not allowed to go anywhere alone. He says he knows how men think and they may go after her. While he is sitting outside the church waiting for her, he says he sees half the same men from his drinking pub on Saturday nights coming out of church Sunday morning. Most of them married with some young woman on their arm every time he sees them. He says if that's what church people do, he sees no reason to go in there and give them his money.

She called me excited one Sunday afternoon telling me how she cried through the whole service. She said it was as if Jesus was personally speaking to her. "I went to the front and told the preacher I want to give my life to God. Michelle, it felt so good," she told me. I was happy to hear her news.

I don't go home as often as I should. They are only an hour away. I put so much time and effort into pleasing Richard, I let everyone important to me slip away. I only visit every few months for major holidays and birthdays. I was afraid of my father as a child. He yelled most days about something. My mother managed to protect my sister and I from most of his violent rampages. She took many beatings meant for us. She always managed to divert his anger back to herself. I love her so much. It hurts me to see how she still does everything for him after the way he treats her. I pray for them nightly. Pray my dad stops drinking. Pray he finds Jesus. She believes in standing by her man no matter what happens. She thinks Richard is a god because he doesn't hit me and come home drunk every weekend. She, like everyone else, thinks we have the perfect marriage. I'm going to have a hard time explaining to her why Richard and I separated.

Everyone thinks we're the perfect couple, everyone but Angela. How am I going to forgive Angela? Jesus says we must forgive. I look up as if looking to the heavens.

"You are going to help me with this one." Forgiveness is the farthest thing from my heart. What I feel now is hatred more than anything else. How can I get past this? I know what the Bible teaches about people who do us wrong and we should love and forgive them. I want to do so many things to Angela right now and forgiveness is not one of them. This is going to be hard. I live in the same town as she and Richard. I will see them eventually.

My mind starts reciting all the things I wish I had said to them. I want to tell them the kind of person I think they both are. The anger I feel. The hurt I could have inflicted if my mouth had opened. I know God kept me, but that doesn't mean I didn't want to hurt them the way they hurt me.

"Thank you, Jesus, for keeping me." I can't always control my thoughts, but I need help with my actions.

If I had been able to open my mouth, there is no telling what would have come out. What actions it would have led to. It would have only made matters worse and made me feel no better. They sit under the same pastor and hear the same Word of God as I do. Why does it have a different effect on them? I could not do what they did to a stranger and definitely not a friend, my best friend. I know it is going to take the power of God to keep me from saying what I want to say. I want to call and unleash on them, Richard first. Get him out of the way first. His pain will be the easiest to deal with. I stopped trusting Richard a long time ago, but I trusted Angela. I close my eyes and allow my mind to run over all the things I wanted to say. I exhale. What good would it do? It won't change the past. It won't make him love me. Won't take away my pain. I try to think of something else.

Pastor. I could talk to the pastor. Uh, I'm not ready to talk to him. He may understand and has probably heard similar from other members, but he has enough on his plate. He stays busy with church stuff and something is going on in his marriage. I don't know if his wife travels for work or church, but she is rarely at church. That can't be healthy for any marriage. In fact, I have not seen her in over a year. I don't know if it will do any good telling him anyway. I would mainly be doing it to tell on Richard. What good would that do? I need an encouraging word from someone. I may talk to him later. I must deal with this alone, for now.

I walk out of the bathroom and look around our house. Everything I look at brings the flood of emotions back. My marriage is over. Richard left me. If he comes back, will I take him back? Am I ready to be single? Should I go ahead and call a lawyer? I can't deal with this now.

I don't want to think of Richard. My eyes fill with tears again. I think about my trip that afternoon. I could use that getaway right now. I don't trust myself to drive that far and don't want to be around people.

What am I going to do? I need to get out of this house but go where? My whole world is work, church, Angela and Richard.

I go in my room. Nothing in my room is about Richard. There is a picture of Angela and me hanging on the mirror. We took it on one of our trips to the movies. We ate at Stranton's that night. She loves Stranton's. I take the picture and rip Angela out of it. I don't know if I will ever understand how she could do this to me. I know she likes different men, some of them married. It never crossed my mind that she would sleep with mine.

She has her choice of men. Many of whom will marry her instantly. What is it about Richard? I told her he is good in bed, but that was the extent of it. She gave detail about several men that went far beyond what Richard and I did. I may never know how their relationship started. Maybe I don't need to know.

I need to think of something else. I pick up the remote and turn on the radio. My favorite song comes on. Jesus by Shekinah Glory Ministries. I smile. I need to hear this. Jesus is my everything. God is so good. I lay on my daybed and hug three pillows. The tears begin to flow. The song seems to lay over me like a cloud. I allow the music to minister to me. JESUS. I love the name JESUS. There is something about that name. It eases my pain, my confusion, my anger. I know I am not alone. The song lasts for over ten minutes. And for ten minutes, I feel Jesus cradle me in His arms. My tears dry and I feel peace in His presence. The peace that comes from knowing I am loved. Somehow, I know I am going to make it through this. I can do all things through Christ which strengthens me. I can heal. I can smile. I can love. I can forgive. I may not feel it at this moment, but I can with the help of my Savior. I don't know how anyone makes it through this life without Jesus.

"Thank You." I look toward the ceiling. "I love You too."

Chapter 6

"Mrs. Moore. Mrs. Moore."

Johnathan waves his hand in the air to get my attention.

"Yes, Johnathan," I call on him.

"How can we love our enemies, when they keep being mean to us?"

Johnathan Port and his mom, Vanessa, joined the church about two months ago. I have never seen a more curious child. He makes my Sunday School class more interesting. I was worried I would be too distracted to teach this morning, but when I looked up and saw twelve smiling faces, my heart melted. I teach the nine through twelve-year-old age group. They are the highlight of my week. I love teaching. If you want to be challenged in the Word of God, try teaching children. They ask everything. If it comes to mind, they will ask it. Johnathan takes the question asking to another level.

"We love because Jesus tells us to love," I reply.

Our Sunday School lesson is titled 'Love Your Enemies' from Matthew 5:38-48. When I began to explain verse forty-four, 'But I say unto you, Love your enemies, bless them that curse you, do good to them that hate you, and pray for them which despitefully use you, and persecute you;' Johnathan's hand goes up.

"Why should we love them if they don't love us?" If Johnathan thinks of a question, he asks it.

"We love because God is love and He wants us to be like Him." I can't help but feel my words as I say them. Loving Richard and Angela is going to be hard. But Jesus commands it and with His help, I believe I can do it. I am not there yet, but I must believe I can.

"But if they're mean to us, we should be mean to them. My daddy said if someone cursed me, I should curse them back. And if they put their hands on me, I should ball my fist up and punch them in the nose as hard as I can."

I pinch my nose to suppress a smile. I have never seen Johnathan's father at church. His advice is going to make teaching Jonathan a little harder.

"Johnathan, I understand your father wants to teach you to defend yourself. But that is why we come to church. We want to learn what Jesus would do. We want to live like the Bible teaches us and not as the world has taught us." I can see he's thinking. I love his inquisitiveness. He is going to make a great Bible student one day. His questions make it hard to get through the Sunday School lesson in forty-five minutes though.

"Why should I listen to Jesus and not my dad. I have never seen Jesus. I see my dad every day."

OK. This is about to go away from the lesson, but he asked.

"We listen to Jesus because He is God, creator of everything, including you and me. He is Lord over everything in the earth and He left His Word for us to learn what He wants of us. And He knows best."

"So how do I know this is God's Word? Anyone could have wrote it." He barely lets me finish the first answer.

I love this kid. His questions are genuine, and I believe he is sincerely trying to understand the lessons. He has an active mind and his mouth is fast to follow. I smile realizing the lesson on the love of enemies is shot, but the class will still get a good lesson today.

"God's Word has been proven over the years. Since the time of Moses from the beginning of the Bible, the Jewish people, whom God chose to be His people, have kept the books and laws of God in written form. For them, the Word of God is precious, and they don't want to lose it. This means it is the most important thing they own, so they protected it over the years. They taught it to their children as I am teaching you and passed the writings along for others to read." I began explaining.

Johnathan's hand goes up. "My dad says the Bible is just a book written by man. He doesn't believe all this God stuff.

"Your dad does not have to believe it for it to be true. Maybe he just needs to be taught how to recognize God. In the Old Testament, before Jesus came, God spoke to men called Prophets who told the people what God said. After Jesus, in the New Testament, His disciples and others wrote down what they witnessed, which is what God wanted us to know. God left us a written word to help us understand Him."

He is listening as if trying to understand all I am saying.

"The Bible is not one book, but sixty-six different books written by around forty authors over more than fifteen hundred years. All the men who wrote the books of the Bible are inspired by God. No one person could make all those books come together to tell the amazing story of creation, sin, God's chosen people, the coming of Jesus and the end times without the help of God."

"I hear you, but how do we know what to believe?" Johnathan and the whole class are attentive.

"You listen to your heart. God works through the heart. Your heart will show you the kind of person you want to be. God is good. The feeling you get to do good comes from God." I continue. "God will deal with your dad when He is ready. Prayerfully, he will become a believer also. You should invite him to church with you. One day God will do something in your life, and you get to decide if you want to believe in Him. He does this for everyone. I am to train and teach you in the ways of God and hopefully when He speaks to you, you'll recognize Him, say yes and accept Him in your heart. He will do the rest through you."

I don't know if they understand me, but all the student's eyes are on me.

"Did that make sense?" I ask the class.

Most of the class nods. Before I could go back to the lesson, there goes Johnathan's hand again.

"Yes, Johnathan."

"How did it become one book then?"

You got to love him. I smile.

"Years after Jesus and His Apostles died, many church bishops got together took the Old Testament writings of the Israelites and the writings of the Apostles and those who followed them and put them into one book as the authoritative Word of God. Over the years, it became the Bible we use today." I hope this satisfies him on this subject.

Nope. His hand goes up again.

"Johnathan, we are actually on a lesson about loving our enemies. I can get us a lesson together for one of our Wednesday Bible Studies. We can do an in-dept study on where the Bible comes from and have handouts for you to take home. That will give us more time for questions."

He smiles. "I was going to ask how you know all this stuff?"

"Years of studies and asking questions as you are doing," I tell him. "I love God and love learning about His Word. I pray you all soon feel the same."

His hand goes up again. I look at him and lean my head to the side. He puts his hand down and pinches his lips together.

"Let us continue," I say.

* * *

I arrive at Harthwell's on Monday determined to bury myself in work. I still hurt all over and did not get enough sleep. I know with time; I will feel better. For now, I just want to crawl in a hole and never come out. I missed a day and a half last week, so I am behind. I dive into my work. I hope no one addresses me today. I don't feel like conversating. Work distracts me. I focus and complete twice as many reports as normal. I avoid conversations as much as possible. Somehow, I manage to smile and speak to keep from being asked questions. Only a couple of people notice something is different. I tell them I have a lot on my mind, and they don't pry.

By Wednesday, my stomach still feels sick and hollow, but my workdays are feeling normal. I still didn't have an appetite. I force myself to drink juice to keep some form of nutrients going through my body. Occasionally I feel the tears form in my eyes. Managing my thoughts is still very hard. There is so much I want to say to those two. There is nothing here at work to remind me of Richard. I decide to take my trip planned for the weekend before. I need a change of scenery.

"You OK? You have been awful quiet this week." Qamar sticks his head in my cubicle.

He startles me. I'm lost in my thoughts.

"I'm getting there," I reply.

"Is everything alright?" he asks.

I pause and look at him. I debate what to tell him.

I decide to give him a general update. I want half the day off Friday and need his approval.

"Can I finish this report and come in your office?"

He gives me a concerned look. "Sure." He turns and walks away.

I walk into his office about thirty minutes later. I look at the floor and then at him.

He doesn't say anything. He stops writing and lays his pen on his desk. Leaning back in his chair, he gives me a concerned look.

"Hey." I pause.

He nods but doesn't say anything. I get his apprehensive look.

"Richard and I split up."

"Why?" He asks more as a reaction than a question. He looks at me waiting for more info. Qamar didn't know much about Richard and me. He met him at a few Christmas parties and of course we looked like the happy couple. He can tell I'm struggling to continue.

"Well, is it the argument split up or the I'm done with you split up?" he asks.

"He found someone else," I tell him.

"Whoa." Qamar is on his third wife, so he understands relationships and breakups very well. "That's awful. What are you going to do?"

I have decided what I am going to do but I am not ready to say it out loud. I cannot spend another night in the same house with Richard. I convinced myself to wait one month before going to a lawyer. I want my mind clearer and I want more time to pray and hear from God.

"For one," I tell Qamar, "I want half the day off Friday. I had planned a trip this past weekend and then all of this happened. I need to get out of here. So, I plan to go to the beach and relax a little."

"Sure. Take all the time you need. I knew something was wrong. You are quiet but never that quiet," he says.

"I'll be fine. Things in our relationship have been going south for a while. I should have seen this coming. I just want a change of scenery. I'll be back Monday refreshed and ready to work. I've caught up most of my accounts, so I won't have a mess to come back to."

"Sounds good," he says.

I can tell he is done talking. He picks up his pen and goes back to his work.

"Thanks." I walk back to my desk feeling uplifted. The thought of getting away for a few days makes me feel better.

* * *

I arrive home that evening excited. One week down and I have not lost my mind. I am going to make it through this. My mind still has not fully processed all that happened but I'm moving forward. I'm going to the beach this time. I am not going to allow Richard Henry Moore III to bring me down. I stop at the drive-through for supper. I need to eat something. Richard hated it when I stopped. He always wanted home-cooked meals. It didn't matter how tired I was.

It's the middle of August. I'm taking my bathing suit and get in the water. Smiling. I sit at the table and remove my grilled chicken sandwich from the bag. I hope this doesn't upset my stomach. I still don't have much of an appetite. The beach. It feels good to have something else to think about, something to look forward to.

I hear a noise at my front door. The doorknob jiggles, then hard. My heart begins to race. I hear a loud banging on the door. Frowning I walk to the door. I look through the keyhole to be sure. Exhaling, I open the door keeping the chain attached.

"You changed the locks?" Richard yells.

I tell myself to stay calm as I walk to the door. I knew this day was coming. I would have to face Richard sooner or later. I look at him through the cracked door. He steps back and angrily crosses his arms.

I step on the porch and close the door behind me. "Yes."

"Why would you change the locks on our house?"

"This is my house. Your name is nowhere on those papers. Remember, when I saw this house eight years ago, you told me this was all on me." I am much calmer than I thought I would be. "In fact, you have not helped with one payment. Your name is not on anything here. You paid for your truck and I made sure my name was not on it. By the way, good luck when you need help with those payments. Your only contributions were for utilities and half the time something came up and you couldn't pay those. At least now I know where your money was going."

"I am still your husband. I can come and go as I please."

I did not move away from the door.

"Not for long. And you can go where you please, just not in here," I reply.

He glares at me. "What does that supposed to mean?"

"Your things are in the garage."

This past week has been hard on me. Each time I mustered up the strength to move forward, I saw something, and the tears started again. By Saturday morning, I made up my mind that Richard is in my past. The first thing I needed to do was get his stuff out of my house. My initial inclination was to burn everything. After my debate with God, my Spirit said "no" to that. Richard did not have much in the house. His clothes, shoes and personal items in our room. Most of the pieces in his man cave were gifts from me. I wanted to burn those too. Of course, I heard "pack those also, you gave them to him, it's just stuff." God's Spirit is powerful when we listen to it.

My argument. Seriously. He gets to treat me like dirt, and I must be nice and do the right thing. I don't want the stuff; I just don't want him to have it. He should buy his own stuff.

Silence. I get silence when I already know the answer to my argument.

OK.

The more I obey, the better I feel.

I spend most of Saturday moving his items. As I start packing, I'm angry at all the money and years I wasted on him. With his truck gone, I move all his items to that part of the garage. I pack his suits, all of which I bought. His Cooper Drink Dispenser. It has a beautiful curved design and complimented his man cave. He only used it for beer which made me hate I bought it. Waste of two-hundred dollars. The Two-foot Mock Cruise Ship from our third-anniversary cruise. He wanted one for a souvenir, so of course, I buy it. Cuban Cigars in a case that cost more than the cigars.

The tearing starts when I get to the plaque from our sky diving vacation. For our first anniversary, Richard wanted to go sky diving. He said it had been his dream since a child. So, I contacted the resort, booked our flight to Hawaii and there we go jumping out of a plane. I was scared but would have done anything for him. That vacation was what our honeymoon should have been like. Richard was happy and he made sure I was happy also. When we walked on the beach or ate out, he held my hand and looked into my eyes as if I was the most important part of his world. The resort captured a picture of us in the air and framed it in an engraved plaque. It was Richard's dream, so he kept the plaque.

The first five years of our marriage were not so bad. I'm not sure what sparked the change, but soon things started a downward spiral and never got better. Richard spent less time in church, less time at home, and less time with me. I cough to clear my throat and wipe away the tears. A lie. All a lie. Back to packing.

His grille rarely used. It had rollers so it was easy to get in the garage. He only cooked on it when he had friends over. He spent most of his time away with them. The hardest thing not to burn was his prize possession Dallas Cowboys Fan Chest displayed in the corner of the room. His dream was to play for the Dallas Cowboys. For a store promotion, if you bought the complete chest you were entered in a contest for a signed jersey from Dak Prescott, Dallas Cowboys quarterback. I bought the chest and Richard won. The oak chest is beautiful. Blue and silver everything packed with the foam number one hand, pom pom shakers, cap, flag, football, mug, umbrella and more. He displayed his signed jersey over the side of it. It cost me five hundred dollars. I really wanted to burn it, but I wouldn't. I couldn't. My heart is not designed to hurt people, no matter how much they hurt me. Even though my flesh wanted to, I learned to listen to my heart long ago. As much as he hurt, I can't purposely hurt him. But I refused to allow him to hurt me again. He's going to regret letting me get away. I did everything for him.

"I want to go inside and talk," Richard says snapping me out of my thoughts. We are still standing outside my front door.

"We have nothing to talk about. You made it clear I was never who you wanted. I have accepted that and prepared to move on." I break eye contact but regain it quickly. I am determined to stay strong through this. There is something I want to know.

"How is Angela?" I ask. She hurt me, but I can't help being concerned about her wellbeing.

"She's recovering," he snaps. Then his expression softens. "They couldn't save the baby. She had surgery Saturday. That trip wiped us out. That specialist we went to see did not take Medicaid. We had to pay him three thousand dollars just to see her. Then he told her there was nothing he could do. I have been off work all week taking care of her."

I chuckle. The thought of Richard caring for someone other than himself almost made me laugh.

My expression relaxes. I know she really wanted the baby.

He looks me in the eyes and reaches for my face. "I just want to be able to come by and check on you sometimes. I know you will need company every now and then."

I step back. Rage goes through me. Does he actually think he is about to get money out of me?

"I'm fine." I push his hand away.

"Well, if you could let me borrow about five hundred till Friday, I'll pay you back."

My brain can't even process this. I look down and then back at him. I guess he thinks I am considering it. He smiles at me. I am just trying to get my words together so I don't say something I will regret later.

"I do still love you," he says.

"Do you really think I'm that stupid?" My voice comes louder than I want it to. My plan was to get through this without a fight. Something in me snaps.

He frowns and gives me a surprised look. I continue.

"You walked away from your 'cash cow' after getting only thirty-five hundred dollars and you call me stupid."

"What are you talking about?" he asks.

I shake my head. And he calls me stupid. "You walked away from the best thing that has ever happened to you and that's all you asked for. I would have given you any amount you asked for if I had it. Ten-grand would not hurt me. Yes, I have it and more. I have other investments and a nice savings that you don't know about because you never talk to me. I would have given you anything. Not because I am weak or stupid. But, because I am a Godly woman who wants, wanted her marriage to work. I was praying you would someday come around and see what a jewel you had. But that ship has sailed. So, please get your things and leave. It's all there. If I forgot something text me and I'll sit it out front."

The only thing missing was his love seat. I couldn't move it alone. If he wants it, I'll get someone to help me move it out. He stares me in the eyes, with his mouth open. One eye is half closed as if he's thinking, contemplating.

This is a look I have never seen on Richard. He looks as if his favorite team has lost the national championship and he thinks he can magically switch the plays to change the outcome. I turn to walk back into the house.

"Maybe I could come by and, you know, visit you sometime." He softly grabs my arm to stop me.

"And now you think I'm going to pay you for sex?" I bark. "I guess that is what I've been doing our entire marriage. Well, that stops now. You know what that makes you if I have to pay for it don't you."

His eyes widen and he glares at me. I pull my arm away and walk inside locking the door behind me.

Leaning against the door with my eyes closed, I feel my heart racing. I must admit, this feels good. I can't remember talking to Richard that way. I feel relieved it's over.

This is the first argument Richard has lost to me. I guess he realizes it. Here comes the yelling, insults and profanities.

"You'll be back. Nobody wants you. I'm gonna make you beg, and it'll cost you more than ten thousand too. You won't find another man who looks as good as me and especially not as good as me. You'll see. I don't need you. Me and Angela will be fine. You're the one with no friends. I have friends to help me."

I hear him in the garage throwing things around. I want to open the door and match his insults but don't. I smile and walk to my room.

Chapter 7

"Hello."

I look up to a shirtless man greeting me holding two drinks. Even with muscles flaring and a bright smile, I'm not impressed.

"Hello," I say unenthused and look back down at the plate of fruit in front of me. I am sitting on the terrace of DeShaun's Bar & Grille. This Friday night's weather is beautiful. I didn't want to stay in my condo and miss the clear skies. The stars are breathtaking. The beachfront properties are aligned with lights glistening off the water. I can gaze at this for hours. I was enjoying my evening until approached by this flat stomach over-eager smile.

"Mind if I join you?" he asks.

I didn't want to be bothered. I instinctively look around to see if there are any other empty tables. The place is packed.

I try to look pleasant. "Sure."

He slides one of the drinks in front of me.

I push it to the middle of the table. "No thank you."

"Please," he says. "No strings attached."

"I'm fine," I say pointing to the diet sprite in front of me. "I don't drink."

"I can refill the water or whatever it is you're having."

"No, thank you. This is enough. I won't be here much longer."

I came here to be alone, not to be pestered by some over-enthused fiend.

"Don't leave on my account," he says. "My name is Mike."

Mike looks like he's in his late twenties. He reaches across the table to give me a handshake.

I look at his hand for a second. I don't want to give him the wrong idea. I am not in the mood for this. He looks great. About five feet eleven with light caramel skin recently oiled to glow. His muscles are not as defined as Richards, but it's obvious he takes very good care of his body.

I reach over and give him a light handshake. "I'm Michelle." I look down and realize I am wearing my one-piece bathing suit from the pool earlier, with my shawl tied around my waist. Most of the women here are wearing much less than I have on. I guess, sitting alone, I look like an easy target.

"So, where you from Misty?" he asks.

"It's Michelle, and I'm from Virginia."

"Oh, I haven't seen you around here before. I would remember you."

"I didn't say where in Virginia."

He leans forward on the table. "Why would someone as fine as you be sitting out here alone?"

Here we go. How do I get rid of him without being too rude?

"Because I chose to." I think he can see I am getting a little annoyed. Being hit on was not on my vacation agenda. I have not thought of sharing a bed with any man other than Richard for fifteen years and I do not want to think of it now. I still feel dirty from learning I paid for sex for that long.

"Mike, I don't mean to be rude, but I just come out of a relationship and I simply want some me time."

"I completely understand that, although, I don't see why any man would let you get away."

Do women actually have to deal with this daily?

"Mike. I'm a Christian woman and I believe God will put the right one in my path when He is ready." Maybe talking about God will get rid of him. This is one subject most men do not want to talk about. But I am not so lucky.

"I am too," he exclaims. "I know God. How do you know God did not send me to you?"

I'm fully annoyed now. I pause to keep from saying the wrong thing.

"Because God knows me. He knows I don't drink. He knows I'm still married, and He knows what type of man I like." I give him a finalized look. I hope God knows what type of man I like because, at this point, I have no idea.

He looks as if he is thinking. He is not leaving without giving this his best try. Almost like I just gave him a challenge that he must accept. I get the feeling he is not accustomed to hearing no, especially from a woman who clearly does not look his equal.

"You said you are not in a relationship, didn't you?" he asks.

I nod. "But I am married."

"But you are separated?"

I stare at him without responding.

"And you said you are a Christian?"

"I am," I respond.

"So, if you are not in a relationship and I am single too, what is wrong with us hooking up to keep each other company. Too many people use God to block people from enjoying life. I know God loves me. God is not worried about two adults having fun. He made us this way to enjoy each other." He looks at me with a 'top that' look.

My annoyance turns to anger. He's actually using God to try and get me into bed. Breathe Michelle. Is this even worth trying to explain? Probably not. I look at him.

"He sure did write a lot about fornication in the Bible to not care," I say.

He's irritated now but he still won't leave.

"But I don't see anything wrong with two people enjoying each other. We are both adults. We can go back to your room and forget our problems together. You'll enjoy it. I promise. How do you see that as wrong?"

"A better question is," I say as I annoyingly stare at him. "How do you see it as right? You don't know me. I could have a disease."

"I have condoms," he replies quickly.

I laugh to keep from screaming. Is this all men think about? A quick score.

"The mouth?" I point to my face disgusted.

"We don't have to kiss," he says.

I push back in my chair to stand and leave. He can't seriously think I'll sleep with him after all this.

"Geno. Geno, I know you didn't." A woman walks in the room yelling angrily. With long brunette hair swaying down to her hips and a body like a model, she is heading our way. She is wearing a shoestring two-piece bikini revealing more than I would ever show in public.

Mike jumps to his feet. Before I can stand, she makes it to our table.

"I thought you were headed back to our room with a headache," she says yelling in his face.

Everyone on the terrace looks our way.

I smile. This should be interesting.

"What are you talking about, I was just asking her if she had something for a headache."

Her head snaps to look at me. I cross my arms to my chest and lean back in my seat to cross my legs. She angrily looks down to my feet then back to my face. Our eyes met. I have an unintimidating approving smile on my face. She can tell from my expression; he is lying, and I'm not interested. She turns her attention back to him. I did not even see her hand move, but I heard the slap she put across his head. I almost laugh.

"What was that for," he asks ducking his head. He starts to walk away. She is behind him fussing and shoving him in the back.

"You're lying. Every time we go somewhere you find a way to chase other women."

"You lied too," he protests. "You said you would be dancing with Julie at the lounge till one."

I guess Mike, Geno or whoever he is will get what he deserves. Of course, if she knows he cheats and still stays with him, she can't care too much. I look at the almost nonexistent swimsuit she has on again. What reason would he have to cheat on her? I shrug my shoulders. Why do men do most of the things they do? I stand and head to my room. That's Richard's kind of woman. Maybe I should send her his way. I smile at the thought.

I get to my room and lay on the sofa. I pull out my Bible to read for a while then finish Charlette Green's 'Apple Of My Eye' before I go to bed. I smile at the thoughts from my evening. It is nice to get attention from another man, even if it is unwanted attention. Who knows, maybe one day I will be ready to date again. I do not want to think about that now. Read. Get some rest. Tomorrow morning Norfolk Botanical Garden then back to the beach.

The remainder of my vacation is peaceful. My appetite has somewhat returned so I order the Fish Taco Snack from DeShaun's after leaving the beach. I love fish. Richard can't stand the smell of any seafood, so I rarely cooked it. It is delicious even though I am only able to eat half of it. This is my last meal before I head home. I stand and walk to the edge of the terrace. The ocean is beautiful as the sun glistens off it.

"Beautiful. Peaceful."

It's around five pm. The place is not packed yet. This is nice. I am not ready to leave but the waitress said everything gets packed and wild on Saturday nights. I'll pass on that. If I leave now, I'll arrive home around seven. That will give me time to settle in and get ready for church in the morning. I need to read over my Sunday School lesson again anyway. I am not teaching, but I like to be prepared just in case. With one more walk down the beach; I get on the road to head home.

* * *

I feel refreshed driving home Saturday evening. The weather is beautiful. The sun is setting below the horizon. I must remind myself that I'm driving to keep from being mesmerized by it. I'm glad I took this short trip. I needed it. I see many more in my future. The scenery. The people. The food. The beach. The atmosphere. All at my fingertips, yet for the past ten years, so far away from me. Although the pain and bad thoughts are still here, I also feel hope for a normal future.

Single life. What will it be like for me? My life has been Richard for so long, I don't know what I want for myself? When I try to think about it the pain intensifies. I know this pain will go away with time and prayer, but for now, I don't know how I am going to deal with this.

Do I revert to my maiden name? Ms. Michelle Francesca Hill. Yes. I don't want any part of Richard. I need a clean start. But, where do I start? What do I have to look forward to? What is it I want to do? I try to think of the things I enjoyed before marriage. Nothing exciting. Before college, most of my free time was spent with Angela. I went places with her I didn't enjoy. I only went because she wanted to go. Then I went off to college. College life was boring until I got in the choir. Now church is a part of my life but what else is there. What do I like to do now? I like reading. The occasional movie. Cooking, but that was mostly because I had to. God, I'm boring. I spent so much time making life to please him, I forgot about pleasing myself.

That is about to change. I begin to focus. Before I arrive home, I will have at least three life-changing to-do items to stimulate my life forward. There must be something I like to do. I've tried hanging out with friends from the office, but it usually leads to drinking and conversations that are not interesting to me. Then I get bored and want to leave. Not to mention Richard hated it. Now that I am separated from him, I will hang out with my co-workers more. Richard says they are high-class and snotty. I think he just hated not being the center of attention. Since much of our conversation centered around work, he was clueless as to what we were talking about most of the time. I told them 'no' to invites so many times, after a while, they stopped asking us out. Most of them are decent people. Many Christians. I'm sure I can put forth more effort to interact with them. How else will they get to know me?

One of Pastor Collin's favorite lines on fellowship is 'to make friends you must first show yourself friendly.' How can they know I love them if I am never around to show it? I will even spend some of my lunchtime with them. I like my alone lunchtime to read so I will alternate between them.

Hanging out with co-workers cannot be one of my life-changing events, but it will help in the transition. My family is much the same. I love them but talking about God is not in my family vocabulary. Maybe it should be. We have a great time when we're together, but most of our gatherings involve dancing to loud music, drinking and smoke-filled rooms that make it hard for me to breathe. Richard likes our family gatherings. We would only attend two or three times a year, which he looked forward to. They saw him as the bigshot in the room. I don't know why. I need to see more of my family. How can I draw them to Christ if I am never around? I'll add that to my to-do list, but still not a game-changer. This is sad. God had to remove my husband for me to see how much I am neglecting His people. I should be a light for Him. If they never see me, how do they see the changes He has made in me. I will do better.

More travel is absolutely one of my life changers. At least once a month, I am getting away, somewhere, if only for the weekend. I can try different restaurants while traveling. We always ate where Richard wanted to. Vacations. I have time off accumulated at work. At least two vacations per year. A cruise. I love cruises. I have only been on one and it was amazing to look out over all the sea. Yes. Two vacations, maybe three. My brain is starting to work. I feel hopeful. Only two of my life changers to go.

Maybe I can do more at the church. Other than pleasing Richard, this is the only thing I found satisfaction in. I can do more with the kids. But what? I'm already on the rotation for Sunday School and Bible Study. We could plan more trips with the kids. Yeah. I love those kids. More local outings for them to invite friends and family to join in on the fun. They need more interaction with church activities. And they need to see we can do more than the once a year outing, we take them on. I can take my class on small trips. I have money saved. Since I am not wasting it on Richard, I can put it to positive use. The church also has a fund set aside for the kids. I will talk to Pastor about it. This will be good. Feeling enthused, my mind begins listing places we could go. I smile to myself. Only one more. This life planning is easier than I thought.

"It's time." I feel pressure in my chest. I frown looking around the car to see where the voice is coming from.

"Michelle, it's time." My entire body feels as if it's wrapped in a soft cloud. I feel heaviness all over. A peaceful compression. Soothing yet firm. I pause to see if it will go away. It doesn't.

I hear it again. My heart warms. This is a good feeling. I recognize the voice, but I'm confused about the message. I wait.

"It's time for you to preach My Word."

"Huh." My heart rate increases. "What? Wait. Wait. Wait." I don't want to hear what I'm sure I heard.

"Preach My Word. This is your call into ministry." His voice is clear.

My breathing increases to match my heart rate.

"Seriously? Now? Are You sure it's me You want?" I try to protest. "But. Wait. I'll do more at the church. The kids. I'll work more with the kids. I will, I have plans to."

I feel the pressure slowly releases me. He's gone. I stare straight ahead. Speechless. I inhale and exhale deeply several times. I don't want to preach. There are so many who want that spotlight. Let them have it. I see so many ways this can go wrong. All the people who will be against me. But how do you say no to God? My mind is contemplating every excuse I can think of. I begin to blurt them out as fast as I can.

"No one is going to listen to me. We have preachers on every corner. Why do I need to do it? The district leaders don't allow women preachers in the conference. I do not agree with everyone and will offend some. I'll join the choir. I can sing, a little, in the background. My life is messed up right now. I need to figure out what I'm going to do about my marriage. I don't like the spotlight. There are so many others more qualified. I have only taken a few classes."

Silence. Eventually, I stop the excuses. I guess I forget who I am trying to convince. I know I have lost. God has spoken, and I am not going to change His mind. I love my church, but church people are something else. Some of the worse personalities I know sit in church every Sunday, yet everyone in there is convinced they are sealed by heavens grace. Most have their minds already made up and there is nothing anyone can do to change it. For too many, the church is not to learn about God, it is to learn how to get what they want from God. What can I do with that?

A preacher. A female preacher at that. Most female preachers I know started their own church to have a place to preach. Why does it have to be me? Maybe my ministry will be something other than standing behind a pulpit? There are so many ways I can benefit the church. But He said, "preach His Word." I guess I should have known this was coming. With my developed boldness to stand in front of crowds and my love of teaching His Word, He has been building me for this a long time. In school and college, I was shy and insecure. I couldn't make eye contact with anyone I was speaking to and panic-stricken if I had to stand in front of the class to speak. Now He wants me to stand in front of a bunch of self-absorbed men who feel I am wrong to be there. An appointment from God should be amazing. Why does it make me feel so awful?

God called me. I was visited by the Almighty. I felt His Spirit all over me. This is amazing. Why can't I feel good about it? What am I so afraid of?

God is love. Everything I believe about God and His Word is built on the foundation of His love. We may all operate under different premises, but the output should be the same, love. Most of what I see in the church is not love. Am I to try and change people's mind, when most don't want to change? And why should they? They believe they have received the prize of eternal salvation. The way I see it, if I don't look like a runner, act like a runner and never get on the track to run, why train if I've been told over and over that I have already won the race. Why change if I don't have to become who I say I am? What can I do about that mindset?

Over the years, God has made me strong and certain of who I am and who's I am. No one can make me feel less than I am. God has made some amazing changes in my natural and spiritual life. I love to teach others how to receive more of what He has to offer. The main thing my fifteen years of experience has taught me is, most church people are happy with the way they are spiritually. They don't want to grow in God. They want more stuff. Better health. Better relationships. Better positions. But, allowing God to work through them to be a living witness is something many have no desire to do. The strong point of the ministry God has given me is showing others how to be more like Christ. How do I give people something they don't want?

This is the reason I love teaching children. Kids are innocent, pure. They're curious and listen with enquiring minds. Even if they stray from the church, I have the chance to impart knowledge and love to them at an early age. Some of it will follow them to adulthood. Misleading them at a young age can have devastating effects later in life so I take pride and care into what I teach them.

How is Pastor Collins going to feel about this? We have never had a female preacher in our church. Pastor Collins has stated several times that he believes God can use anyone, but I know two of his associate ministers do not believe women should be in the pulpit. With the district being against it, I don't want to bring undue pressure on him. He works hard to keep confusion out of the ministry.

Pastor Collins is a good man and he is very involved with what happens at the church. He occasionally leaves the men's Sunday School class and comes and sit in with the youth. Most of the time he's silent or only offers a few words of encouragement. Sometimes he visits our youth Bible Study class in the same manner. He says it is important for the kids to know their pastor cares for them. The kids love him. They will not leave the church without giving him a hug. Every youth outing or function, he is there or sends word why he must miss it.

Our church has over five hundred members. He has his hands full overseeing the many areas needed for the church to function. He allows each department head to operate on its own, but he likes to be involved and informed in all we do. All the department's major decisions must be approved by him.

He often reminds the department leaders, "you represent what the church stands for, the church represents what I stand for, and I represent God. Anything we do as a church is a direct reflection on God and His message to the world. So, I hold myself accountable for this ministry because God positioned me as the overseer of His sheep."

How is my pastor going to take this? His hands are already full of everything else that's going on in the ministry. Some people in the church are constantly stirring up problems. The last thing I want to do is add to his burdens. He has associate ministers, deacons, missionaries, and others to help, but this decision ultimately falls on him. I know God called me, but this will affect him as much as me.

"What am I to do now?"

"Go talk to your pastor. He will direct you." I hear His voice as plain as if I am talking to a person.

I exhale. I am not getting out of this. When should I go talk to the pastor? Silence. I look at the time. I have an hour until I get home. It will be around seven. Should I go by the church? He spends most of his time there. I don't want to bother him, but my instructions are to tell him. He is busy most of the day on Sunday. Maybe it will have to wait till next week. I will swing by the church on my way home. If he is there, I'll tell him. If not, it will have to wait.

Oh, why me? I hope he's not there. I drive for the next hour in silence. Reflecting on what has just happened and wondering what this all means for my life.

Chapter 8

"Come on in." I hear as I softly knock on the pastor's door. He had to be here. Pastor Mark L. Collins. I read his name tag on the door. Does this man ever go home? OK, Michelle. You can do this. Just turn the knob and go in. My hands shake as I push the door open. He looks up from the book in front of him. His eyes light up. A big smile comes across his face.

"Sister Moore!" He stands and walks around to greet me. "What's the good news?"

He throws one arm around my shoulder and pulls me in for a hug. I somberly return his embrace. Stepping back with his enormous smile, he awaits my answer. Why does he think I have good news? Most people don't come to the pastor with good news. I come to his office, unannounced, at eight on a Saturday night, and he thinks it's good news. What did he see when I walked into the room? I know how I feel. If my face reflects the way I feel, I look panic-stricken and desperate. I try to match my answer to his reaction, but I can't.

I pause and look down at his shoes. You can do this Michelle. I bring my eyes back to meet his.

"Hello, Pastor Collins. I have been," I pause. Breathe. "I was returning from the bea... God spoke to me." Spit it out, Michelle. My eyes began to wander around his office. He sees I'm struggling with something but patiently waits. He keeps a soft smile on his face. I clear my throat. I can do this. I look him in the eyes.

"God called me into the ministry." There. I said it.

He stands there and looks at me for about five seconds. It feels like five hours. His smile widens. He pulls me into a full embrace.

"It's about time. I knew you had the calling. This is good news. This is great news. Yes."

I pull away from him with a confused look on my face.

"But I thought the district does not allow women preachers?" I ask.

"Some in the district may not, but they do not oversee this ministry. God has placed me over this church, and I follow God's lead above man's." He walks back around his desk to his seat. He points to the empty seat in front of his desk. "Have a seat. If you say God has called you into the ministry, and I believe He has; it is my job to help prepare you for the awesome responsibility He has given you. Let me worry about the district, and you focus on allowing God to use you."

I feel a huge weight lift off me. "Thank you, Pastor. That went much better than I expected."

"I could tell you were nervous. When you walked into the room, there was a glow about you. I knew I was about to get some exciting news. Being called by God is very exciting news. There's no need to be nervous. It is a great responsibility, but I believe you are up to the challenge."

I look at him still not convinced. "I'm glad someone's excited about it."

He smiles at my reaction.

"I mean, I love God and I love helping in the ministry. But preaching. Me, preaching? Don't we have enough preachers?" I say.

"When God called you, He knew what He was doing. You don't have to persuade me. I can't get you out of it because I didn't call you into it." He gives me a comforting smile. "It's a natural feeling to not want to stand in front of a crowd and preach God's Word. Ministering a great obligation. Not only are we responsible for what we say, but we're also responsible for how we act, how we treat others and how we respond to the way we are treated. When God calls us, He's not just calling us to speak His Word, He's calling us to 'be' His Word; to be a representative for Him on earth."

Whoa. I stare at him processing all he is saying.

"When we say yes to God, our lives are put in the spotlight. Sister Michelle, you've been living this life for a long time. I've watched you develop over many years. You love God, you live God and you represent God well. Who better to put out front to be an example of His Word?"

I sit processing all he is saying. Never thought of it that way. He continues.

"Preaching God's word is just a way to extend the ministry God has placed inside us. Yes, we must study more. Yes, we must meditate and pray more. But all of this is because we want to be the best we can be for God. When we accept a call into ministry, our life is no longer about what is important to us. It is about what's important to God and to His purpose. Your ministry will not and should not be like anyone else's. I can only guide, but God will develop you into the minister He wants you to be."

I lay my head on his desk.

"Oh boy. Something else to add to my plate."

I hear him chuckle and I sit up.

"You are going to be fine. God qualifies who He calls. He will take care of you. And, He gave you some great leadership to help along the way." He pauses so I can realize he is talking about himself.

I smile at his attempt to humor me. His smile fades and he gives me a serious look. After a short silence, he speaks.

"Michelle, is everything all right with you?"

Shocked by the subject change, I don't know how to answer. Am I ready to have this conversation with him?

He continues. "First, you missed Bible Study last Wednesday. When you came in Sunday, you performed your duties well, but you obviously had something else on your mind. Again, this Wednesday you were here at Bible Study, but you didn't seem yourself."

He noticed all that. He is paying more attention to us than I thought. Well, it is his job to watch over his flock. I look over at a stack of books on the corner of his desk. Then at the note pad with notes scribbled on it. When I start to pick my fingernail, he speaks again.

"We all have rough patches in our lives. Believe me, I understand those. Just know I'm here if you ever need to talk."

I'm ready to talk about this. To him. He is about to mentor me as a preacher, so he needs to know what he is taking on. I slowly raise my head to make eye contact. There is that reassuring smile. I feel warm. Peace. Safe. Free to share my burdens.

"Richard and I separated." The words flow off my tongue. It feels strange saying it to him.

"What?" He asks shock. "I thought you guys had the perfect marriage."

I guess God doesn't show him everything.

"Most people do. Richard worked hard to keep up the charade in public. In private, our marriage has been headed downhill for a long time."

"What happened if you don't mind my asking?"

I can feel the tears forming and tightness in my chest. My stomach begins to turn. I look down. You can do this Michelle. You are done crying over a man who never loved you.

"I caught him in our bedroom with another woman."

His eyes widen. I clarify my statement.

"They were not intimate at that moment." I continued. "But it was clear they had been. They soon confirm it."

He nods. "Men are, well, we're stupid sometimes. I'm sorry. I mean, sometimes we do stupid things. We are weak and we don't always think with our brains."

"Have you ever cheated on your wife?" I snap sarcastically. I feel bad as soon as the words come out of my mouth, but still insulted by him defending an unfaithful husband. Pastor Collins does not seem like the type of man to cheat on a woman. Not all men cheat. I could be wrong though.

"No," he proclaims. "When we married, I loved my wife very much. I believed she was my soul mate. The idea of cheating on her never crossed my mind. But that does not mean over the years the temptation has not presented itself. Too many men lack the discipline and spiritual growth to fight the temptations we all face daily. When Jesus saved me, God did something in me that I can't fully explain. Although I struggle and fall short in some areas, in other areas, it's like a line is ingrained in me not to cross. Being unfaithful has never been an option for me. When I married Sherrie, I vowed to stay faithful. Faithfulness to God helped me keep that vow."

He looks at me to see if I understand what he has explained. I nod in agreement. I notice he is speaking in the past tense about his wife, but I do not want to point that out.

"I know what it means to have lines drawn by God that we can't cross without serious consequences. I thank God for those lines. They have kept me out of a lot of trouble. I loved Richard when we married and thought he loved me. He made it clear that he never loved me and only married me for the money. He is angry because he didn't get a football scholarship and said I was decent enough to give him a good life."

I wipe the tears away with the back of my hand. Pastor Collins hands me a tissue.

"Wow. He said that to you?"

"As plain as I am speaking to you. Only he had more anger in his voice. Like he blamed me for all the bad things that happened in his career. In his life."

"That had to hurt," the pastor says.

"Not as bad as who he was with." If I am going to unload, I may as well put it all out there and maybe he can help me through the healing process.

"Do I know her?" he asks.

We hold eye contact for a while. I can't get her name to come out of my mouth. If his look of compassion reflects my pain, I look like I'm in a lot of pain. And at this moment, I am.

"Angela." Tears fill my eyes. I can't hold eye contact when I said her name.

"I thought you guys were best friends?" he asks shocked.

"We were."

"Whoa. That is a hard blow for anyone. I don't care how long you've been saved." He pinches his lips together. I guess this is to keep his opinion to himself. He looks at me as if he is contemplating his pastoral words carefully. "Have you decided what you are going to do. The church has marriage counseling and restorative programs."

"You can't repair something that was never together. I did want to talk to you about it. I know what the Bible says in Matthew chapter five about the man putting his wife away because of fornication, but what if it's the man who's doing the fornicating? And in First Corinthians chapter seven where it talks about the unbelieving husband is sanctified by the wife. Also, the part about not putting away an unbelieving spouse if they want to stay. But Richard is a believer, according to him. He wants, how should I put this, he wants to live apart but to continue to come by and 'visit' me when he needs money."

"He wants you to pay for sex?" I can tell that surprised him when it came out of his mouth.

I give a slight nod. "Basically," I say. "I have read over these scriptures several times the last few days I want to do what God's word says, but I can't see me spending another night under the same roof with a man who could say the things he said to me. It makes me sick at the stomach to think of how long this went on without me noticing and even sicker to think of him touching me again. What should I do?"

He drops his head and shakes it. "He has a lot of nerve. So many men searching for a good woman and he has a great one and just throws her away."

His voice is low, but I hear what he says.

He pauses for a second. "I am both Richard's and your pastor. I would like to sit down with the both of you for consultation before you make any major decisions if that is all right with you."

"I am fine with that, but I can't speak for Richard. I'll call him and see if he agrees."

"That's good. And if you can't get him to agree to come, let me know and I'll give him a call."

"Yes, sir." He smiles at my response.

I can tell he is trying to keep his personal feeling out of this, but he is struggling to do so. He looks away. Although much of my pain has returned, this conversation is going better than I thought it would. When he looks back at me, pain is all over his face. Does he feel my pain, or is this his own? He stands and walks to the corner window in his office. It's dark out so I'm not sure what he's looking for. What is he thinking? Does he believe me? Why would I lie about this? He has probably heard every lie in the book and wants to make sure before advising me.

He returns to his seat. Exhales. He opens his drawer and pulls out a manila folder.

* * *

He places the manila folder in between us but I am not sure I should touch it.

"I have also read those scriptures on marriage and divorce many times lately. Sherrie and I have been separated for five years. She sent me divorce papers to sign a month ago."

"Whoa," I say. I did not see that coming. "We all assumed she liked to travel and was following her career path."

"That is what she told several ladies and it's somewhat true. I am just not a part of her chosen path. She has been asking for a divorce for years and I have always convinced her to delay any actions. I guess she got tired of delaying."

"What happened, if you don't mind my asking?" I give him the same question he gave me. "Of course, you don't have to answer if you don't want to."

He looks at me for a minute as if contemplating his words. I can tell he is not accustomed to being on the receiving end of the questions. At fifty-two years old, Pastor Collins is a stunning man to look at. He has this stern masculine appearance that makes him look intimidating if not for the softness in his eyes. Not to mention the soft smiles he gives everyone he approaches. He keeps his short-boxed beard neatly trimmed down his sideburns. Backed by a medium golden complexion and deep amber eyes, sometimes I must remind myself not to stare. One can easily get lost, mesmerized by his presence. His voice snaps me out of my assessment of his appearance.

"Our marriage started out great. We were young and in love. We had been together for over six years, so marriage seemed like the next logical step. After living together for three years, marriage just made it official. We were inseparable. A beautiful couple. I was her king and she, my queen. We partied and hit clubs, together as husband and wife. We did everything together.

"Neither of us were in church. I was raised in the church but never took any of it seriously. After college, I convinced my mother I was too busy for church. My mother is a very devout Christian and I love her dearly. She is my biggest fan and supporter. My dad was a good man, but he did not like to come to church. I wanted to be like him. But mom never gave up on me."

He smiles as he talks about his mother. He references her in several of his sermons and teachings. She is a major contributor to the man he has become. He continues.

"After Trey, our firstborn, turned one, we occasionally took him to church to please Mother, mostly on Mother's Day, Easter and

Christmas. She was so excited to see him. She loved her grandson. We had a free babysitter too."

I can see he enjoys the memories. My heart becomes heavy at the thought. I want children and because of Richard, I never got the chance. I push the thought of him out of my mind. I want to listen to his story as he has listened to us so many times over the years.

"Church stayed the same for us after Shantell, our second child, the occasional visits. But when Austin, our last child came, I really began to reflect on the type of father I wanted to be; what I wanted my children to see and remember about me. I felt drawn to church, but I resisted the urge at first. I started taking the kids to church every couple of months. Sherrie would go sometimes. She did not like to go to church. She says my mother didn't like her. I told her Mom just didn't like the fact that she couldn't cook."

He laughs. "How can she raise kids if she can't even turn on the stove." He mocks his mother.

"I told her the kids ate healthy, wholesome meals. My mother worked as a chef and taught me to cook and I later developed a passion for cooking fancy meals like her. I made sure the kids ate wholesome meals; only the occasionally take out."

He exhales and gets to his point. "One Sunday morning, the kids and I went to church. Sherrie did not go with us. After a spirit-filled praise and worship service, the preacher asked three members for a testimony. I was feeling something that service. I didn't know what it was. I remember standing on my feet, clapping my hands through a few songs. Most of the congregation was on their feet so I didn't feel out of place. It felt good. My mom was the third member to stand after the pastor asked for the testimonies. She thanked God for all He had been for her over the years. My father passed when I was fifteen. She never remarried. I can't even remember her having a man at the house other than family. She finished raising me alone. With help from the church, we managed to make it. We didn't have much, but we were happy. With tears in her eyes, she praised God for being with us through my teenage years. She admitted not knowing how she would raise a teenage son alone, but then pointed at me."

"Look," he repeated her words. "With the help of God and my church family, I was able to keep him off the streets, off drugs and from being shot." Her tears flowed freely. "God gave me a second job, and I was able to get him through college and back home to me. He could have moved anywhere but told me he would never be far from me. Now he's married with my three beautiful grandchildren. When I looked over and saw him on his feet praising God, I knew my prayers had been answered. God is working on him. I couldn't sit quietly any longer."

His eyes form tears as he recites his mothers' words. He catches himself before they run down his cheek. I am captivated by his story. I don't want to interrupt. I can tell it feels good to be able to share it with someone.

"Instead of being embarrassed by my mother's testimony, my heart warmed. I reached over and wrapped my arms around her and almost lifted her off the floor. I was not sure what I was feeling, but I wanted more. When the preacher opened the doors to the church, I stood with Austin in my arm. He was only a year old. I took Shantell and Trey with my other hand and we went to the front of the church. Mother sobbed the whole time we were there.

"This is when things began to change at home. I went home excited about my new faith. The kids were excited about being in front of the church and the newfound attention they received. The youth minister and youth teachers made such a fuss over them, I think they were more excited to return than I was. Sherrie wanted nothing to do with it. She made it clear the kids and I could go but she had no desire to start going to church regularly.

"I didn't want this to affect my marriage, so I continued to go to clubs and parties with her on the weekends for a while. The more parties I attended, the less interested I became. On Sundays, the kids and I were in church. When I came home eager to share something I learned, Sherrie didn't want to hear it. We slowly drifted apart. Soon she started to go out by herself. She saw I wasn't enjoying myself and suggested I stay home.

"I tried to do what the pastor suggested and be the good husband and father to draw her to God, but it didn't work. She enjoyed being with the kids and me for all our other family activities, but she wanted nothing to do with church. She would attend the kid's presentations at church, but that was about it."

I can tell this is painful for him to talk about. His eyes have been on the folder in front of him for the past five minutes. Only making the occasional eye contact.

"Sherrie is not a bad person. She has a good heart. She is a good mother to our kids. She has always been a respectful wife to me, she just did not want anything to do with God. Our interest split us, and only God can repair something like that. I tried hard to understand her resistance and couldn't. She finally admitted why.

"She told me as a child, her Aunt Roselyn, I think she called her, was the Godliest woman she knew. She loved everyone and would do anything for anybody. She said she loved her and enjoyed going to church with her. When she was ten, her Aunt Roselyn learned she had breast cancer. She watched her suffer for two years. Her aunt prayed. The church prayed. They even had Sherrie praying and believing God would save her. When she passed, Sherrie said there was no God and vowed she would never have anything else to do with Him.

"Me, being a young convert at the time she confided didn't know what to tell her. I tried to get her to talk to the pastor, but she wouldn't. Even after she saw the changes in me and I understood enough to explain, she had her mind made up and refused to listen. Something has a hold on her and won't let go. To keep the peace in our marriage, I stopped trying to persuade her and prayed for God to show her the way.

"After three years in church, I was called into the ministry. I explained to her how much I love her, but I had to do what God called me to do. We talked and wanted our marriage to work. She tried for years to be supportive. I could tell she was miserable, but I prayed. Her life outside the church didn't change but she came to church more. She was there whenever I preached. But we became progressively distant in our marriage.

"Fifteen years ago, our pastor relocated to Nevada for another pastoral position. Since I was being prepared for leadership, I accepted the role as pastor. I was a young pastor, but I was dedicated to serving God. Sherrie did not like the idea of being a pastor's wife. I convinced her to stay with me, but it put an even greater strain on our marriage. Five years ago, she called it quits. She moved out. Our youngest is a freshman in college. When you see her in church, she has come for money. She always has some unexpected expenses he needs help with. She always comes to the church to prevent having to sit down and talk to me for too long. I was not shocked to receive divorce papers, but I wish she would come and talk to me."

I look at him. Silent. I don't know what to say. He looks up at me and composes himself.

"Sorry I unloaded all that on you. I've never talked to anyone about most of that. You are easy to talk to."

"I'm glad you confided in me. You probably get an ear full on a weekly basis from all of us," I tell him.

"Yeah. It felt weird being on the giving end of the pastor's table."

"What are you going to do?" I ask him.

He looks down at the folder on his desk. "I don't know. I need to do some more praying about it."

I frown. "Pastor, I don't mean to be presumptuous. But, if she left five years ago, why would you want to be married to someone who does not want to be married to you? It's not fair to her to be tied to a man she does not love."

I admit I had my own situation in mind when I made that last statement.

"I know," he replies. "And I thought of all that. My issue is not love anymore. I do still love her. I guess a part of me always will."

He looks away for a second, then back to me. "My concern now is representing God and being misleading to my congregation."

I give him a confusing look.

"I have counseled and married countless couples over the years. My advice before and after marriage is to prevent divorce. I have encouraged couples to trust God and go the last mile to keep their marriage vows. Many have stayed together through some tough situations. One member said she cried for forty-five days straight when her husband left for another woman. When he came back and asked forgiveness, she forgave him. They came to my office. We counseled and prayed. Seven years later and they are still together.

"I have held marriage conferences and seminars to help build and sustain marriages. How will it look if the pastor suddenly gets a divorce? Even if it's not my choice. Five or ten years down the road, I can see members justifying divorce because I did it. What kind of message am I sending?"

I look at him. Was that a rhetorical question? He has so much to deal with. Being a pastor is hard. He pauses as if awaiting a response from me. Does he want agreement from me? I understand his dilemma but I'm not the pastor. I'm seriously contemplating divorce. I may not be the best person to ask about this. My mouth opens and words come out.

"Pastor Collins. I understand your reason and respect your will to represent God despite your feelings. But, what about you? You should have a life also. God may have used her to send you those papers to release you. How does it look to the church, associate minister's and members to have a first Lady who is never at church to support her husband? What kind of helpmate image is this giving?"

"I never thought of it that way," he replies.

I continue.

"Church people will surprise you sometimes. If you divorce and don't tell them why you will have every rumor floating around you can think of. But, if you explain to them the basic circumstances behind the divorce, they will understand and respect you more for it. I know I do. I would not advise anyone to stay in a marriage where they are not wanted. The Bible even teaches us to release them if they want to go."

He smiles at me. "You are right, and members do surprise me sometimes. You have given me a different way to look at my situation and pray."

I look at my watch. Eight-forty-five.

"It's late and I need to get home and settle in," I tell him. "We have church tomorrow."

"You're right," he replies. "If you're settling in, where are you coming from, if you don't mind me asking?"

Very perceptive. He has a light peaceful smile on his face. It's as if he wants to continue the conversation.

I smile shyly. "The beach. I needed to get away."

"That is a good idea. I need a vacation myself. I can tell your skin is a little darker. Enjoy the sun?"

I hear him chuckle under his breath. I guess my face turns red from embarrassment. Is he teasing me?

He stands and walks around his desk to face me. I stand to meet him.

"Congratulations on your call into ministry. Stop by my office Wednesday after Bible Study. I'll have you a Ministers Starter Package to get you going. We can talk about that later, there is no rush."

He stands directly in front of me with a serious look on his face. "I won't say it will be easy, but I will tell you, it is definitely worth it. Despite what I just told you, I could not begin to tell you how good God has been to me. Accepting my call into ministry has been beyond fulfilling and I wouldn't trade it for anything."

"Thank you, Pastor." I extend my hand to shake his.

He throws his arm over my shoulder and pulls me to his side. As he walks me to the door, he looks down at me with his arm still over my shoulder and smile. "For the first time, I get to say this."

I give him a puzzled look.

"Thank you for listening to me."

I giggle still a little embarrassed and step out the door. "You're welcome. And could you do me a favor?"

"Anything," he answers.

"Could you wait to announce my call to the church? I need to wrap my head around all of this first."

He smiles. "I'll allow you to announce it when you are ready."

"Thank you and good night."

"Good night, Sister Moore."

More impressive than his physical appearance is his spiritual presence. I couldn't help but feel blessed for being placed under his leadership. I drive home more confident about my call into ministry than I was before I went to see him.

Chapter 9

I pull into my garage a little after nine and hit the button to close the door.

"Where have you been?"

Someone yells at me and scares me. I drop my purse and hit my head on the car door frame while getting out. I didn't see him walk through my garage door before I closed it. I stand up rubbing the top of my head. My heart is racing uncontrollably. He yells again.

"Richard, what are you doing here?" I'm angry and yell to match his.

"I've been over here five times today. Where have you been? You were not answering your phone."

I turned my phone off. That was the whole purpose of getting away. I wanted to leave my life behind for a nice quiet break. My heart slows to its normal pace, but my anger increases.

"And I asked you, what are you doing here?" I stare at him with the same intensity he is giving me.

"I need to talk to you." He tries to soften his voice. This only means he wants something.

"You could have knocked on the front door like a normal person instead of scaring me like that." I keep my intensity. I want him to know how much I disapprove of the way he approached me. I made a mental note to survey my surround before I drive into my garage from now on.

"Where've you been?" He asks me again.

"Richard, I don't have to tell you anything. You left me, remember. For my best friend at that." I feel the burn in my heart return. Stay calm Michelle. I reach in my car and push the button to open the garage. "Will you leave, please. I'm tired and need to get ready for bed."

"I been gone for a week and you already off laying up with some joker."

"Seriously. You say that to me. If I wanted to lay up, I would bring them back to my house." I feel dirty when that comes out of my mouth. Don't stoop to his level, Michelle. He will say anything to hurt you. Don't feed his anger. He steps toward me. I step back.

"What do you want?" I ask him.

"We need to talk."

"That's fine. Pastor wants both of us in his office so he can talk to us."

"You told him? I should have known you would run straight to him."

"What do you have against the pastor?" I ask him. "He has done nothing but try to help us and everyone else over the years."

"This is our business and you are my wife, not his."

"What are you talking about? You know what, never mind. Just leave. I need some rest." I am not in the mood for Richard tonight. He obviously wants something and I'm sure it's not me.

"Not until I talk to you." He leans against my car.

"If you want to talk to me, we can meet at the pastor's office. We need counsel, not more arguing."

"I don't want to argue." He tries to smile. "I just want to spend time with my wife."

"It does not work that way, Richard. You don't walk out on me with another woman and think you can return when you like. So, what do you really want?"

"Let's go in the house so we can talk."

"No." This is getting frustrating. I look at him. How do I get him to leave? "If you agree to meet me in the pastor's office tomorrow, I will agree to listen to whatever it is you have to say afterward."

"Why can't we talk now?" he asks.

"Because I'm tired and want to go to bed."

"I could join you," he says with a deceitful smile.

The rage that goes through me when he says that makes me close my eyes to keep from saying something that I know I will regret later. "Richard?" He hears the anger in my voice.

"OK. Tell me where you were, and I will leave and meet you at the pastor's office tomorrow."

"Fine. I went to the beach."

"With who?" he asks as soon as I get the words out of my mouth.

I stare him in the eyes. I don't want to answer, but I want him to leave. "I went alone, Richard."

He smiles. That makes me even angrier.

"You walk out on me with my best friend and tell me you never loved me. Then add that you have basically been using me for the money for the past fifteen years. I was hurt. I still am. I needed to get away and try to clear my head."

I see the first sign of sympathy on him since I married him.

"Sorry about that. You caught us off guard."

"I will be fine. Can you please leave now?"

"We can talk about it tomorrow. I will make it up to you." He walks toward the garage opening and stops.

"Sure, you don't need any company?"

"Good night, Richard." I reach inside my car to push the garage close button. He pauses before he steps out of the garage. I don't know what he expected from this visit. I'm sure he wants something, probably money. He is not getting another cent out of me. Fifteen years of me trying everything to make a marriage work. Keeping silent. Paying bills. Taking insults. Isolating friends. Being alone. Laying there when I really didn't want to. And all for a marriage that should never have been.

Tears run down my cheek. Was I really that simple and easy during our marriage? I guess I was. No wonder he feels he can say and do whatever he wants to me and still expect handouts. Regardless, how can he honestly think he can say those things he said to me, and I still give him money. I guess I need to show him it doesn't work that way anymore. I just want to be over Richard and move on with my life. The one thing I agree with him on is, I'm glad we never had children together. I may never get the opportunity again, but at least there is nothing to tie me to him.

I think of all the single women in church, still looking, waiting, praying for a husband. And I am about to divorce mine. Yes. My mind is made up. I am divorcing Richard. Through all my reflections and praying on this, I see nothing that makes this marriage make sence. Nothing he could do or say will ever cause me to love him again. I can't trust anything he says. I'm tired. I'll deal with him tomorrow. I don't want to think about him anymore tonight. But that is easier said than done.

It takes me two hours to fall asleep after his surprise visit.

* * *

Pastor Collins is an awesome pastor. I had to call him as soon as Richard left, and he was able to work us into his busy schedule the next day.

"Thank you for seeing us on such short notice. I received a surprise visit from Richard last night. I had to use your counseling session to get rid of him. I called and told him you said to be in your office at one o'clock. I explained that you had another engagement at three, but you could sit down with us for an initial consultation."

"That's fine," says Pastor Collins. "I bet that was an interesting visit."

"You have no idea," I reply.

I do not want to talk too much about Richard. It hurts when I do. Most of what I feel for him involves me being angry and wanting him in my past. I did not tell Pastor Collins my mind is made up where Richard is concerned. I know he told me to wait before I decided, but I can't help how I feel. I convinced myself to come to the meeting with an open mind. I will listen to what Richard and the pastor have to say. The pastor and I have been sitting in his office for fifteen minutes waiting on Richard. Church dismissed thirty minutes ago, and Richard was in service. He was sitting alone in the back. No Angela, but he was there.

I have not seen Angela since she and Richard walked out of my house. I don't know how she's doing. Did she recover from the loss of her child and the ensuing surgery? Have her stomach pains gotten better? I can't help but wonder. A part of me wants to call and check on her. But what kind of message will that give? She betrayed me. She was my best friend for so long and shared so many happy memories. Then she sleeps with my husband. With enough prayer, the pain will go away, and I will forgive her. We will probably never be friends again. I don't know if I can ever trust her. Yet, I still feel bad knowing she is there suffering and I'm not there to help. I'll ask Richard for an update if I remember?

"Sorry I'm late. Nosy people wouldn't stop asking me questions. Need to mind their own business."

Richard barges into the pastor's office without knocking. He walks to the chair beside me, kissing me on the jaw as he sits. "Hey, Babe," he says.

Pure rage goes through me. I close my eyes for a quick prayer. "Hello, Richard," I manage to whisper.

The pastor notices my anguish. "Hello, Brother Moore." Pastor Collins extends his hand to him. "It was good to see you in church today."

"I know, it's been a while. I'll do better. I have had my hands full lately." He curls his eyes my way. "I don't know what she told you, but things are fine with us. A little rocky, but we'll get through this. I don't know why she thinks we need counseling."

The nerve of this man. I look at the floor to keep from exploding.

"Well, we can talk through some basics and see where to go from there," the pastor says. "Your wife is not happy. She shared some concerns with me, and I want to hear your side of things to help you through any issues in your marriage. Marriage is a sacred bond between man, woman and God. We like to do everything within our power to keep from breaking that bond."

"There are no issues, just a small misunderstanding." Richard looks at me and smiles. I keep a blank look on my face, afraid if I open my mouth, the wrong thing may come out.

"Why do you think there's a small misunderstanding?" Pastor Collins sits back in his chair and looks at Richard.

"There's really nothing to tell. She walks in on me and a friend. Yeah, we were in the bedroom, but nothing was happening. We had our clothes on and she blows this way out of proportion."

Richard sits back in the chair and folds his arms across his chest. He flexes his muscles and has this intimidating look on his face. Pastor Collins looks at me then back to Richard. I keep silent. I want to see where Richard is going with this.

"So, you're saying your wife should be OK with you having another woman in her bedroom?" Pastor Collins asks him.

"Yeah, if we're not doing anything."

"So, you would be OK with her and another man in your bedroom as long as they are not doing anything?" he asks Richard.

"Of course not," Richard yells as if insulted.

"What's the difference?" Pastor asks him.

"If a man is in our bedroom, I know what he wants. And I know Michelle. If he gets that far, he's going to get it."

I close my eyes and look down. Stay calm Michelle. Massaging my forehead, I look up, face burning as if bracing for the torture to continue.

"OK," Pastor says. "Let's move on. Is that all that happened?"

"Why are you not asking her questions?"

"Because she has already told me her side. I want you to have the chance to tell me what you see as the problem."

Richard raises his voice. "I told you, there is no problem. I may have said a few nasty words, but I apologized for that. I miss my wife and I just want things to go back to the way they were. Well, almost the way they were."

Pastor Collins looks at him puzzled. "What does almost the way they were mean?"

"Alright man, I know she told you, so I'll admit it. I cheated. I have been cheating for a while. She knows this. I mean, there is no way she couldn't have known. It's in the open now and I want to move past this. She knows what I want."

"And that's what exactly?" I ask barely able to contain my rage.

"I want things to stay the same, only I won't be living at the house. I'll come by and visit about as often as I was before I left. I was barely at the house anyway. You had to know there was someone else. You are not that stupid, are you? I hardly touched you. I mean, I wanted to keep you happy enough not to complain, and you didn't."

I am trembling I'm so angry. "Richard, you really think you can say these things to me, and I continue to pay your bills and share a bed with you?" I manage to get the words out through clenched teeth.

"Why not, you've been doing it for over fifteen years. You should know, Angela was not the only one. I don't want there to be any more surprises. We have lived this way for so long and I don't want things to change. We had everyone fooled and everyone was happy."

Why does this hurt? I didn't think he could hurt me anymore, but he just did. I feel the tears roll down my face. Pastor Collins has sat back in his chair to allow us to talk. I stand to walk out of his office. I will not sit here and allow Richard to do this to me again.

"I was not happy. I was trying to make a bad marriage work. Now I see I was just wasting my time." I head toward the door.

"Sister Michelle." Pastor stops me. "Please. We need to try and work on this." He looks at Richard. "Richard. You can't expect your wife to accept that you will have other women. That's no marriage. That's not Godly."

"She's been fine with me being gone all the time. Why does that have to change?"

I hold my hand up to stop the pastor. There is no sence wasting any more time trying to repair this marriage.

"Richard, the only thing that will make me stupid is if I accept your conditions. What you saw as a weak wife was a desperate wife trying to give her husband what he wanted to keep him. Well, I no longer want to keep you and you will not get another cent from me."

I continue to stand. I want this over. Richard has lost his mind. We were so distant. I knew very little about my own husband.

"I'm still your husband and we can work this out." Richard has a pleading sound to his voice, but I know it's only because he will miss the money.

"There is nothing to work out." My voice rises and the tears flow freely. "You stand in our house that I am paying for, with your girlfriend, my best friend, laying across my bed. You look me in my eyes and tell me you never loved me and only married me for the money. Now you expect me to continue as if nothing happened.

Well, let me tell you what I want. What I'm going to do. I want a divorce. I'm getting a divorce. I am not asking you; I am telling you. As far as what you want, you should have thought of that before telling me how you've wasted the past fifteen years of my life. Not another day. I will be contacting a lawyer first thing in the morning.

"Calm down Sister Moore. Let's not act hastily. Brother Moore should have the chance to reflect on his mistakes and become a better husband." Pastor Collins stands and draws my attention from my rampage. "Richard, would you be will to go through marriage counseling to help repair your marriage? It does not have to be through me. I know several very good marriage counselors."

Richard looks as if he is thinking. "If it will keep things the way they were, yes. I will even agree to move back into the house."

I open my mouth to continue my argument. Pastor holds up his hand to stop me.

"Richard, that is the point of marriage counseling, things cannot stay the same. Marriage is designed for one man and one woman to stay faithful to each other. You must be devoted to your wife and her only."

Richard thinks again. "If she continues to pay the bills, plus my truck payment, I will consider letting the other women go."

I turn and storm out of the pastor's office. The audacity. This is not a negotiation. This is my life. Who does he think he is? Making demands. The nerve of that man. I can't believe what I'm hearing. It's one thing to say it to me, to think I'm that simple, but to talk in front of the pastor that way. Richard can't really believe that kind of behavior is acceptable in marriage, and that the pastor would sign off on it. How could I have missed this for so many years? I should have made him talk to me more. I would have caught on sooner before I wasted that much of my life. I need to get out of here.

Chapter 10

The parking lot is empty. Only Richard's truck, the pastor's car, and my car remain. I sit in my car with my head on the steering wheel. I need to calm down before I drive home. The sooner I get this marriage over, the better. God understands why I must break my vows. He knows I tried to make this marriage work. I need to go home. I will feel better once I talk to a lawyer.

I hear Richard's truck start up and drive by me. I don't bother to hold my head up to acknowledge him. Thank God he doesn't stop. The pastor's car is on the other side of the parking lot, so I am not bothering anyone by sitting. I hear a light tap on my window. I look up. Pastor. I am done talking about this. I am divorcing that man and nothing's going to change my mind. Pastor Collins motions for me to roll down my window. He sees the anguish in my eyes.

I start talking before the window is a quarter of the way down. "I am not changing my mind. You heard that. There is no fixing someone who thinks like that."

"I know Sister Moore," he says sympathetically.

"Call me Hill. Sister Hill. The sooner I put that name, and everything attached to it behind me the better." I'm angry. I know it, but I can't help it.

"Could you come back to my office for a few minutes please."

"I told you Pastor; I'm done with him. I don't want to hear anything else about counseling."

He tries to stop me mid-sentence. "I know and I won't try to talk you out of your decision. I heard enough and understand why you feel the need to. I want to give you something."

I turn the engine off and hope the car stays cool while I'm inside. We walk back to his office in silence. I guess he wants to choose his words carefully. I use the silence to mount my defense. He can stay married to someone who does not love him, but I'm not going to.

We enter his office. He walks around his desk and points to the seat I was previously in. "Have a seat please."

I sit. I want to list off my defense items, but I keep silent. He opens his desk drawer and pulls out a manila folder. It looks like the same one from the night before.

"I did some thinking and praying after you left last night. I decided to grant my wife's request and sign the divorce papers."

He has a sad look on his face. I look at him compassionately.

"It was hard to do, but I felt a weight lift off me as soon as I signed," he continues. He gives a sad smile. "I kind of had to sign. I couldn't concentrate on my reading, lesson or anything else until I did. It feels strange, but I know it's for the best. I believe it is what God wants me to do and He will work things out."

He opens the folder and flips through several pages. Removing a paper clip holding a business card from one of the pages, he looks at the name on the business card.

"First, let me apologize on behalf of all men. I know I said men do stupid things sometimes, but Richard is a special case. Most men are not that way. They love their wives; they just have a problem staying faithful to one woman. Richard is one of the worse I have encountered."

He pauses and looks at me. I don't know what he wants me to say. I have a hard time understanding how any man can cheat on a woman they truly love. But I guess if I understood men, I would not have let Richard make a fool of me for so long.

"Richard is the only real relationship I've been in. Sorry if I don't have a very good impression of men," I reply still on the defensive. It's not the pastor's fault Richard is a jerk.

"Well, it takes a lifetime to build that kind of attitude toward women and relationships. I'm sorry you went through so much with him. I don't know what happened to Richard, but I will continue to reach out to him. Maybe someday. Sometimes it takes us losing what we have to realize the person we should be." Pastor can find a way to make anything positive. Even with someone like Richard.

I nod in agreement. He hands me the business card. "Benjamin Drake is the lawyer my wife is using. He sent me his card in the divorce packet I received. I have spoken with him a few times over this past month. Divorce is a new arena for me. Members generally stay away from me when divorce is their choice."

I can see this still bothers him. The sadness in his eyes. He looks at the card and continues talking.

"He has been very understanding of my concerns. He attends Graceful Freedom Ministries over in Ohatchee. I met his pastor at several leadership conferences. Benjamin explained avenues my wife could take if I would not agree to the divorce; the difference between a contested and uncontested divorce and answered many other questions. Sherrie is really a good person. She has tried to talk to me several times and I found a way around the issues we needed to address. He says she is trying to do this without hurting me. She just wants to move on with her life. I guess she has found someone else. She would never parade another man in public to hurt me, but discretion will only last for so long. She deserves to be free to move on. I won't hold her back any longer."

It sounds as if he is trying to convince himself more than me. He must deal with so much from the members in the church. We never think about what he endures with his personal life. It always looks as if he has it all together.

"He seems to want what is best for both parties," he continues. "If you choose to divorce, he may be good to talk to."

"If I choose?" I ask with an attitude.

"I'm just saying, don't rush into anything. I know you're hurt and angry but give yourself time to settle down and listen to God. I can't say I understand what you are going through, but I know God is in control. He has a reason for everything He allows to happen to those who love Him."

"What possible reason could God have for wanting you to stay connected to a woman for over five years only to have you sign the divorce papers?" My voice goes up as I ask the question.

I feel out of place asking the question but want to make my point. I give him an aggravated stare. I am thinking about my situation. There is no way I'm staying married to Richard for five months and definitely not five years. His eyes lock with mine and he holds my stare. He looks at me without blinking, as if he is looking through me. Thinking. Receiving a revelation from God or something. No emotion. No facial expressions. Just a blank stare. Did I offend him? Did I offend God? A slight smile comes across his lips. As if he has the answer but is not willing to share. He breaks our stare and looks at his desk.

"God knows what He's doing. Just listen for His guidance and you can never go wrong. Now, I have to get ready for my next engagement." He stands and walks around his desk.

I stand looking at the business card he hands me. My mind is focused on my divorce. I don't know what he wants me to wait for. God is going to have to do some major persuading to prevent me from calling this lawyer. I'll wait for the month as I had originally told myself. He sees me focused on the card.

"Don't worry too much about that," he says. "You'll know what to do when the time comes. Besides, we have a minister to train."

He giggles as my expression go from focused to annoyed. Preaching. That's an even worse thought.

"You'll be fine. God's got you. I'll have you some material soon."

"Have a good afternoon Pastor." I walk out of his door.

"You too Sister Moore."

I hear his door close once I turn the corner.

Chapter 11

I teach Sunday School this morning. It is refreshing to be in front of the kids. Being with them takes my mind off my troubles for a while. After Sunday School, I go in the sanctuary needing a word from God. Pastor Collins looks as refreshed as ever. He addresses the congregation.

"I normally keep my private life to myself, but I was recently reminded by a good friend that my church family is my family also." Pastor Collins quickly cut his eyes at me. "I have some news to share with my family." He looks down at the podium as if bracing himself for a major announcement. Looking back into the congregation with his assuring confidence, he begins to speak.

"I have counseled many of you over the years on how to keep your marriages together. As I look over the church, I see many happy couples who have weathered the storms and stayed together. Know that I am proud of you."

He exhales and continues.

"It is with great disappointment that I announce Sherrie and I are going through a divorce."

Gasps and whispering are heard all over the church.

"I know many of you have been wondering why she occasionally attends church. This is why. Without going into detail, Sherrie and I have been on different paths for a long time and we feel it is best if we go our separate ways. We are still good friends, so please continue to show her the same respect she received as First Lady."

I can see this is hard for him. The whispers in the church continue.

"Please don't think we came to this decision lightly. If there was any way around this, I, we would have taken it."

It has been two weeks since our counseling session in the pastor's office. He finally decides to give the church this announcement. He is much braver than I am. As he strugglesf through his announcement, I sit here thinking; "thank God I don't have to stand there and spill my gut to a room filled with judgmental people." Then it hits me, soon I will be up there, spilling my guts to this same crowd.

I often use my personal experiences when I teach. Will I be the same as a preacher? Kids are one thing, but a room filled with adults. I dread the thought of how they will take the things I say. A call into ministry should be exciting. Yes, nerve-wrecking, but positive and encouraging. Why do I always feel anxious and my stomach turns when I think about it. Trust God Michelle. Those He calls, He qualifies. I know, I'm relying too much on what I can do. God brought me to this, and He will bring me through it.

I bring my attention back to the pastor. He saved his announcement till the end of service. He asks the church to stand for the benediction. He has just finished an amazing message entitled 'Make Ready A People' from the book of Luke chapter one verse seventeen.

"God sent the angel to Zacharias and Elisabeth in their old age to let them know He was blessing them with a child. This child, John, would be filled with God's Spirit from birth because God had a purpose for him; to make people ready for Jesus. Once we receive the Spirit of God, we have that same purpose. As we make ourselves more like Jesus, we should focus on helping others get ready also."

"Go ye into the world and prepare others for Jesus. You are dismissed."

I believe God is sending this message directly to me. I have spent so much time trying to prepare myself to be a good example that I forgot I have the 'Believers Calling,' to prepare others for the coming of Jesus. Pastor always tells us that our lifestyle is the best preparation we can give the world. I guess I need to focus on both lifestyle and words. I exhale and head through the congregation of hugs for my car.

* * *

The next few months are filled with ministerial lessons and study material. I'm first given a packet containing the Church Covenant, Church Bylaws and Church Leadership Etiquette. Pastor Collins seems determined to prepare me for every possible encounter I could face. As soon as I complete one assignment, he gives me another. He says it's not only important to understand these concepts enough to display in our daily lives; we need to be prepared to discuss them with others to lead them in the right direction. He has given me three different study Bibles and recommended several other books to purchase or read online. Many of the beginning lessons were on salvation, baptism and grace. I already understood most of this from previous classes I have taken and church. Then the assignments become more in dept.

He suggests I enroll in winter classes at Wesson School of Theology. The school is only twenty minutes away and they have night classes. He often calls me to his office or pulls me aside with encouragement or advice. I know there will be backlash from some of the men in our district. I see members cutting their eyes at us. I have not announced my calling to the church yet. Pastor has enough to deal with without people wondering why we are spending so much time together. I guess I need to announce it soon before the rumors start. Since his announced divorce, I have noticed several young ladies in church now sitting on the front row with short skirts and low-cut blouses.

I missed my weekend getaway last month. I plan to leave Thursday after work and head for the beach. I need a break. It's too cold for me to get in the water, but the scenery will be worth the trip. Most of the resorts will be empty so I should have a quiet and peaceful weekend. To be a single woman, I suddenly have less free time than when I was married.

I take my call into ministry seriously. I study all the materials given to me by the pastor. I work at Harthwell's, come home and put my nose in the books. I must remind myself to take a break. I often go to him with questions. He most always has the answers. And on the rare occasion, he doesn't, he considers it a challenge to get the answer. Sometimes his answer is a book or website to google. I hate it when he does that. He says I need to know how to investigate for myself because soon people will come to me with questions.

The good thing about being focused on my studies is I have little time to think about Richard and Angela. I have not seen Angela since she and Richard left my house; the day I found them in my bedroom. I occasionally still wonder how she is doing, but I can't bring myself to call. The pain has eased tremendously. I just don't want to reopen the wound or appear weak. Richard has shown me what he does with my weaknesses. I get the feeling he used some of his tactics on Angela. He can be very persuasive when it comes to getting what he wants. My heart won't allow me to believe Angela went after Richard just to hurt me. I may never know how that situation came about. Maybe it's best I don't know.

As for Richard, he and I had a couple of run-ins after he received the divorce papers. When he realized I was serious about moving on with my life, he began to beg. Richard begging. Not a pretty sight. He promises to do better. Monogamy. Staying at home. Attending church. He promises everything he can think of, but I know they are just words.

I can tell he has lost weight, yet he is still breathtaking to look at. I know all his promises are to get me to continue taking care of him. My prayer is to get away from Richard without us becoming enemies.

I can't blame him completely for the way he treated me. I allowed it. I knew things were bad and did nothing about it. I could have demanded he take more responsibility, pay more bills and spend more time at home. He would have been a better husband or left sooner. He is one of those people; the more I gave, the more he wanted. If a person loves you, the more you give them, the more they give to you. Not the case with Richard. He was accustomed to getting his way with me and was not about to walk away easily.

"Michelle you know I'm nothing without you."

"No Richard," I tell him. "You have nothing without me. Instead of wasting your time trying to change my mind, get yourself together and take care of you. You have good qualities about you, and you are going to be just fine. I don't want us to be enemies. It is better to have me as a friend than an enemy. You never know when you may need my help."

I don't think Richard has ever supported himself. He moved from his parents to my apartment. It will take some major adjustments, but he'll manage. Knowing Richard, he will just find another woman to take care of him; which is fine with me.

I call him to my house one evening for dinner. I'm not sure what he expected, but I finally manage to get him to sign the divorce papers. He left angry. Slamming my door and walking across the driveway yelling obscenities. The last I heard of Richard was his truck speeding out of my driveway. That was over a month ago.

Pastor, on the other hand, I hear from regularly. Did you read the book? How are the lessons coming? Have you contacted the school? I know he is risking as much as I am allowing a female minister in the pulpit. He will have to answer to some influential men. The least I can do is make sure I'm as prepared as I can be. I don't complain. He keeps me busy and keeps me out of trouble. I want to excel and be able to answer his questions, but he could slow down a bit. Is this what being a minister is going to be like? I know he only wants me to be the best I can be but, there is such a thing as an overload. Does he put this much on the male ministers? Listening to some of them preach, they didn't pay much attention to the studies they were given. I even wonder sometimes where their sermons come from. It's obvious they didn't write them. Their terminology does not match the way they normally speak, and they miss pronounce many of the words in front of them. Pastor says he did not call them so he can only help prepare them. They are responsible to God for the rest.

* * *

Am I ready for this? The more I learn, the more it seems there is to learn. It's mid-November and I still have not announced my calling to the church. It's time. I will pull Pastor Collins aside after Sunday School and let him know I'm ready to make the announcement. I get nervous at the thought of it. What will the congregation say? What are the associate ministers going to say? Reverend Michael Lewis will be supportive. I think. Sister Glenda, his wife is the other Sunday School teacher for my age group. He and Reverend Daniel McCormick often encourage the women in church to follow their calling. Reverend Kevin Jones and Deacon Mattis Green, on the other hand, make it clear; they believe women should keep silent in church. We should not be allowed to teach or anything according to Deacon Mattis. He said he almost left the church years ago when Sister Rachael was assigned the teacher over the youth, but he convinced himself she was just babysitting the kids. He grew accustomed to women teachers. He says he stayed because his grandfather was the first deacon of this church and he belonged here. It will be interesting to see how he reacts to a woman minister.

I have attended this church since I finished college. It was where Angela attended so I joined. I have never seen a female preacher in that pulpit. This is going to be a big adjustment. Today is Thursday. I have three days to prepare my words to the congregation. I will be fine. I can do this. I did not accept this call from them, but obedience to God. Give me strength, Lord.

This Sunday morning, I do not have to teach the kids. I spend most of the women's class convincing myself to go ahead and tell Pastor Collins I'm ready to make my announcement. I like the way we alternate teaching. It allows us the opportunity to work with the kids and fellowship with the other women in the church. True to his word, Pastor has not told anyone, and he did not pressure me about announcing. I don't know why I am nervous about this. The announcement is the easy part. Preaching in front of them will be the hard part.

I leave the women's class and go through the side door to his office. I take the longer route. That gives me more nerve-prep time. "Stop procrastinating and go to his office," I tell myself. I turn the corner closest to his office and almost bump into someone. I jump and stare into some angry eyes. Before I can step back and speak, a slap comes across my face so hard I stumble backward into the wall. I surge forward and stop when I realize who it is. Shocked. I open my mouth to argue but, her voice overrides mine.

"It's your fault. Yours. You walk around here acting all saved and holy, but you're just a wolf in sheep's clothing."

I stand with surprise and anger in radiating off me. My fists are still balled. I'm confused but before I can launch my attack, she continues her argument.

"You alt to be ashamed of yourself. I am going to see to it that you are kicked out of this church. They were working on their marriage and you were behind the scene keeping him distracted."

"Mrs. Mable. What are you talking about?" I yell angrily. I step closer, flesh still wanting to take over. I'm still confused and trying to convince myself not to attack. She is too fragile for me to touch, but her swing feels like she has been working out in the gym. Regardless, she hit me. Without warning. Without saying a word, she slaps me. She is obviously confusing me with someone else or received the wrong information somewhere. Either way, you ask questions not to put your hands on someone. I stare at her angrily, what is she expecting my reaction to be. I'm sure I startled her as much as she startled me, but I am not sure where the swing come from.

Mrs. Mable Cook is Sherrie's mother, Pastor Collins ex-wife. She is a faithful member of the church and leader of the Missionary Association. She adores Pastor Collins. She could not have been happy when he and Sherrie divorced. My brain focuses on what has her so angry, but I still don't know what she is talking about. I am too angry; I can't arrange my words without attacking. Before I can ask, she attacks me again.

"He is a man of God and you flaunted yourself in front of him till he gave into you. Richard told his mother, Geneva, all about you."

Something inside me explodes when she says his name. She slaps me because of something Richard said. I am about to attack a seventy-five-year-old woman. I forget I am still in the church. My voice is much louder than it should be.

"You slap me because of something you have heard. From Richard, of all people. Have you lost your mind?" I didn't realize I had stepped directly in front of her. Mrs. Mable is taller than me, but I didn't care. She needs to get her story straight before she decides to put her hands on me.

"I see the way he looks at you, everyone does. Something is going on."

"Ladies, Ladies. What's going on?" Pastor Collins walks out of his office.

We are standing ten feet away from his door. He must have heard all the commotion. I look at him, still angry. I notice one of the deacons and a couple of the ushers looking around the corner.

"Step in my office. Both of you."

We follow him into the office.

"Have a seat."

He points to the two chairs in front of his desk; the same seats Richard and I were in for our counseling session.

Mrs. Mable sits in a chair but scoots it away from me.

I almost laugh, but instead, I lower my head and shake it. Feeling a little calmer, I realize she is simply acting on a lie told by Richard.

"Will one of you please explain to me what is going on."

Mrs. Mable looks at me. "Huh." She rolls her eyes and looks away.

I look at Pastor Collins with pain and anger in my eyes.

"She slapped me."

"What?" he replies. "Mother, why would you slap Michelle."

She looks me up and down and rolls her eyes at me again.

"Because she caused you and Sherri to divorce," she says angrily.

"Mother, Michelle had nothing to do with our divorce. Sherrie and I have been separated for over five years and she asked me for a divorce. I didn't want to, but I had no right to hold her back any longer."

His eyes were sad and filled with sincerity. His mother looks at him with surprise.

"You know Sherrie won't talk to me about her personal life," his ex-mother-in-law said. "She says I'm always in her business and trying to tell her what to do. I knew something was wrong. She is never at church. No one has to work every Sunday."

"It's fine Mother. What happened with Sherrie and I was for the best. She and I are still good friends."

"Well, Richard told his mother that he thought you and Michelle had been together for years. And you know Geneva, she told everyone that's why he and Michelle got divorced."

"Richard," I growl. "I'm going to..."

Pastor Collins holds up his hand to stop me. Rage goes through me. Pastor Collins can tell I want to explode. He gives a slight shake of his head for me to stay calm. I try to compose myself. Mrs. Mable continues.

"Everyone could see they were a happy couple and we wondered why they suddenly got divorced. There were rumors about Angela, but then Richard told his mother what happened."

She gives me another evil look. I covered my face with my hand and leaned over my knees. My face is hot. I feel something wet on my thumb. Blood. Somehow, she scratched me on my lower jawline. I straighten up, exhale and rub the blood between my fingers. Anger is all over me. Anger at her. Anger at Richard. Anger because I can't say what I want to say. I growl out some words.

"Mrs. Mable. Richard and I had problems for much more than five years. He only wanted us to look like the happy couple. He is angry because I will no longer support him, so he will say about anything." I shake my head. "How could he make up a lie like that?"

"Mother," Pastor Collins looks Mrs. Mable in the eyes. "There is nothing, nor has there ever been anything inappropriate, going on between Michelle and I. Richard or someone lied."

"But you two spend so much time together. Everyone has been whispering about how much you talk and we're not blind. You can't keep your eyes off her."

Our eyes lock. He holds my stare for a minute then drops his head. I guess he is searching for words. I have no idea what she is talking about. I know he is monitoring my studies, but that is it.

"Sister Michelle is working on something, but it's her news to share, not mine." Pastor Collins looks at me to continue, but I can't get the words to come out. After what she just said the whole church thinks of me, I can't stand up there and tell them I've been called to preach. They'll think I am the biggest hypocrite. I look down at my hands.

Mrs. Mable stands. "Well, I believe you, Pastor. If you say there is nothing going on, then there is nothing going on." She pats me on the hand. "I'm sorry I slapped you, dear." She walks out the door.

What just happened? I can't stay angry at her for worrying about what the entire congregation thinks of me. How will I face them? I just want to go home. I look up at Pastor. I can't even process what just happened. There is no way I can make that announcement now. He stands and walks around his desk to face me. When I stand, I am only inches away from him. With a tissue from the box on his desk, he extends his hand to my face and washes away the blood. I forgot about that. This feels strange. Awkward. Scary. Good.

I take the tissue from his hand. His touch is soft.

"I'm sorry," he whispers.

"For what, you didn't slap me."

He smiles. "But I caused you to get slapped. What were you coming to see me about?"

"Huh?" My mind is not functioning. He is standing much too close to me. I feel his breath on my face. I take a step back to concentrate.

He never takes his eyes from mine. "You were outside my door about to beat up my mother-in-law, so I assume you were coming to see me about something."

"I was not going to hit a seventy-five-year-old lady, I don't think."

He laughs at me trying to explain away his joke. "I know you wouldn't."

"I'm glad one of us knows," I say looking unsure.

"She had just left my office asking me about Sherrie. I told her she needed to ask Sherrie. Maybe I should have explained more to her. I was not thinking the rumors had gotten so bad." He lifts my chin to look into my eyes. "You still didn't tell me what you were coming to see me about?" He is still standing over me looking down with those soft amber eyes and inviting smile. I can't concentrate. I must look away to answer. I got caught up in one man's looks before and it cost me fifteen years of my life. I am not falling for that again.

"I was coming to ask if I could announce my calling to the church today, but that's out the window. Most of them think I'm a floozy who caused your divorce. They'll look at me like I'm crazy."

"Do you trust me to announce it and try to straighten some of this out?"

How could I not trust that face?

"Yes." I manage to say the word but I'm sure my face said much more.

"Don't worry about this. Continue to live your life with integrity. It will speak for you and dispel all rumors."

"I hope so," I whisper. My mind is torn between Mrs. Mable's words that he can't keep his eyes off me and how the church will react to the announcement. My desire is not to fall for another handsome man, and he is drop-dead gorgeous. When does this get easy? I seem to continue to be punished for trying to do the right thing.

"Ok. Let's go. We have to go and start service." He places his hand on the small of my back and leads me to the door.

I feel a tingle go from my lower back to my head then to my feet. I close my eyes as I step through the door opened for me. Oh God, not again.

Chapter 12

I walk into the sanctuary unable to make eye contact with anyone. The pianist is softly playing 'Leaning on the Everlasting Arms.' I can't make it to my usual, right section, second-row seat. That will require me to walk across the front of the church. I stop on the left and walk down the side aisle to the fourth row. It's empty. I sit down and open my Bible to distract myself. It feels as if every pair of eyes in the sanctuary are on me. I'm sure some members heard Mrs. Mable and I arguing in the back. They must think the worst of me.

Pastor Collins enters a shortly after I sit. He opens service with his customary 'Call to Worship.' Maybe he will wait till after his sermon to address the church. This will give the congregation time to focus on something other than me. After greeting the leadership and congregation, he addresses the rumor.

"Since I announced my divorce from Sherrie, many of you have been wondering what lead to the divorce. It is natural to wonder. That is part of our nature. But I told you, my church family, all there is to tell. Sherrie and I want different things out of life. We tried. We just could not find a way around our differences."

My heart is racing as he makes his announcement. It is hard for me to look up at him. I know almost everyone is watching my reaction. At some point, my name is going to come into his speech. He is calm and looking into the audience with compassion.

"I hear rumors that Sister Moore, I mean Sister Hill had something to do with my divorce. That is not true. There is nothing, nor has there ever been anything inappropriate going on between Sister Michelle and me." He looks at me with a soft smile and gives me a slight nod.

"Who knows what the future holds," he adds. His gaze softens and he slowly turns his attention back to the congregation.

My heart feels as if it is going to jump out of my chest. What is that meant to imply? Is he suggesting he wants something more with me? I hear soft murmuring across the church. I drop my head. I can tell my breathing is heavy. I must get myself together. This is just the beginning. If I am to stand in front of this crowd, I should be strong enough to take the good with the bad. People talk. They have opinions and sometimes make up stories to go with those opinions. I knew this would not be easy. God has shined a spotlight on me, and I must trust He will give me the strength to stand in it.

Give me the strength to allow You to shine through this. I am more than a conqueror through Christ Jesus who strengthens me. I slowly turn my head to look around the congregation. Most are looking at me. There are mixed expressions on their faces. Most don't know what to make of this announcement, but the pastor is not finished yet. He clears his throat and continues.

"Sister Michelle came to me several months ago and announced her call into the ministry."

He paused after making this statement. All eyes turned directly on me. After a moment of silence, loud mumbling spread across the church. He taps the mic to call the church to order.

"For me, this is great news. Sister Michelle is an invaluable asset to this ministry. She displays God in her daily character and lifestyle. I think God made an excellent choice calling her to represent as one of His chosen vessels. She asked me to wait to make the announcement to the church. As you can imagine, this was news to her as it is for the rest of us. However, when God speaks, we must act accordingly. She accepted His call and came to me for instructions on how to proceed. Over the past few months, she and I have been preparing for her upcoming endeavors in the ministry. She came to my office this morning prepared to make the announcement. I believe she is ready to walk in her new calling."

He looks at me with an encouraging smile. I force myself to smile in return. I'm coaching myself inside my head. Keep eye contact. Don't let them see you sweat. You can do this. You're ready. On the outside, I want to get up and run out of the church. He continues to address the church.

"I know some of you have objections to female ministers. Understand, God does not have respect of person. God does not see gender when it comes to the Spirit. He calls whomever He pleases and qualifies us for the work of the ministry. I am very proud of Sister Michelle for accepting His call and look forward to mentoring her as she grows in her calling."

With his announcement over, he precedes through service as normal. I hear mumbling across the congregation for a while then things settle down. I don't hear much of what is said after that. I look at the ministers sitting behind the pastor. Reverend Lewis looks at me with a big smile. He gives an approving clap in my direction. Reverend McCormick smiles also. However, he looks around the congregation as if worried about their reaction rather than standing on his own convictions. Reverend Jones frowns. He won't even look at me. He looks as if he wants to walk out of the church more than I do.

I don't look around the congregation. I hear the whispering, but I am prepared to deal with them. I feel confident knowing Pastor Collins supports me. It is he I will rely on the most.

My mind wanders during most of the service. The announcement is made. I can only look forward from now on. I force thoughts of fear and regret from my mind. Although I am angry, I will not approach Richard about the lie he told. Richard is in God's hands, and I plan to leave him there. It will do no good to argue with him anyway. The congregation will be filled with questions. I'm not sure how they will respond to this new change in the church. Forty percent of the congregation is over sixty-five and they have the most influence of how the other's respond. The subject of female preachers has rarely come up in our conversations. It will be interesting to see the reception I receive. Today, I just want to get out of here and get home. To safety. To seclusion. To quiet. To gather my thoughts and prepare myself for what's to come. This has been a very eventful day and it is not even twelve noon.

I watch the pastor during his sermon. He is passionate about his preaching. I don't know a more dedicated person to the work of God. My mind wanders to his statement concerning us "who knows what the future will hold." I'm not ready to get into another relationship. Richard did a number on me. At one point, I loved him. I worked hard to show it. If marriage is this much work, do I want to consider it again? Pastor Collins is not like any man I have ever met. Does that mean he will make a good husband? Maybe I am reading too much into this.

I close my eyes to shake the thought of him out of my mind. When I open my eyes, he's there. Mic in hand. Preaching with conviction. Sweat runs down the side of his face. I focus on his words.

"Be not deceived; God is not mocked. Whatsoever a man soweth, that shall he also reap."

His words resound in my Spirit. I look down at my notes to see his subject and scripture. 'Reaping the Harvest. Galatians chapter six verses seven through nine.'

"If we put out love, love will come in return. If we put out joy, joy will come in return. If we walk in peace, peace will follow us. God is not just promising to build our finances, and natural possessions; He wants to build who we are. If we put out the characteristics of His Spirit; love, joy, peace, longsuffering, gentleness, goodness, faith, meekness and temperance; we will reap the benefits of His love, His joy, His peace, His longsuffering, His gentleness, His goodness, His faith, His meekness and His temperance. Don't expect man to give you what only God can. Man can only operate in God's Spirit and through God's power."

Pastor can bring God's word to life. I will never be able to expound on God's Word the way he does. He finishes his sermon and the choir erupts with a beautiful rendition of 'How Great Is Our God.' Caught up in the praise, I almost forget my adventures of the day. As soon as Pastor Collins stands to dismiss church, they all come flooding back to memory.

I prepare myself to head toward the exit as soon as he dismisses. Since I'm sitting on the opposite side of my normal, I must cross the church to get to the exit near my car. I mentally route my escape path. Pastor dismisses. Pastor always step-down front to greet members as we leave. I cross behind the chairs set out front for the invitation to join the church before he can get into position. Reverend Lewis catches me before I can get across the opposite side. I almost made it. Ten feet from the door. He embraces me with a big hug.

"Congratulations Minister. You got it in you. Welcome aboard." His smile is genuine. It feels good.

"Thank you, Reverend. I welcome any pointers you can give me," I tell him.

Glenda, his wife, walks up beside him and gives me a hug. "You are going to make a great minister. The kids look up to you. I know they like your teaching more than mine. A couple of them told me. You know kids, if you want to know the truth, ask them."

"This is a big step from teaching kids," I tell her.

She hugs me again. "You can do this. Think of all the young women watching and being impacted by your life. You can open the door for so many of them to follow."

I had not thought about that. Reverend McCormick is standing behind them to greet me. His reception is much the same. He welcomes me to the ministry. I see Reverend Jones walk out the side door. I can tell he is still not happy about the announcement. I look up and there is a long line of people, mostly women, waiting to greet me. My heart swells. It is a good feeling. A smile is on every face in the line. The hugs and congratulations come one after the other.

"Sister Michelle." I turn to see Pastor Collins calling me. Our eyes lock. He has a warm smile on his face. "May I see you in my office before you leave?"

I strain to hide my expression. Nerves. Tension. Excitement. Exhaustion. I need to get out of here today. I nod to him. The thought of being alone in the room with that man again today is more than I want to handle. I turn to face the next person in line. They are all very accepting of my calling. I receive genuine love from my fellow worshippers, and it feels good. The response is much greater than I expected. I catch a few eyes roll at me. Others walk out without saying anything. I am prepared for negative feedback. If I can just make it out of the pastor's office without falling apart, this will be an oddly successful day.

* * *

"Come on in," Pastor Collins says to my knock. I don't know why my heart is racing, but it is. Maybe the adrenaline from the official announcement of my calling. But I think part of it is the idea of being alone in a room with this man. He is a man. An impressive man. A pastor, yes, a distinguished pastor. But he is also a man. Human. Flesh. With needs. The same needs as every other man. Clear your head, Michelle. I am not ready to deal with this feeling, whatever it is. I must concentrate on my calling, but I need to spend time with him to get the proper guidance. The upside is, the more time I spend around him, the less I think about Richard. This is going to get interesting. I must lean on God for guidance now more than ever.

Pastor Collins is writing something when I enter. I go to my customary seat. He lays his pen down and walks to the seat adjacent to me. I get the feeling he is about to talk to me instead of the 'talk at me' feeling I usually get when he is behind his desk. My body tenses uncontrollably.

"You have had a busy morning," he says with that inviting smile. The smile that makes my head spin.

"That's an understatement," I say trying to return his smile. I encourage myself to make eye contact. He leans toward me. This man even smells good. His looks are mesmerizing. I hope he doesn't realize the effect he has on me. I was fine around him until his ex-mothers-in-law statement. 'He can't keep his eyes off me.' I wish she had not said that. Not in front of me. Not now. I have always placed him in that category of gorgeous, Godly men who are out of my reach. Therefore, he has never been a temptation. Knowing what I know now, I can't seem to keep the thought of him out of my head.

"How are you doing?" he asks me.

He can tell I'm struggling with something. I pray he doesn't realize it's him now. Get it together Michelle. You don't even know if he is interested in you. Tell that to my mind and body. I exhale and focus on the matter at hand. My call to ministry.

"I am fine, or I will be. This too shall pass. Right."

"Yes, you are correct. I have faith in you. So much that I have chosen a date for you to give your trial sermon."

My heart jumps. I look at him with widened eyes. He smiles.

"Don't worry. You've got this. You embody everything it means to be a Christian. The most important thing I can teach you about addressing the congregation is to approach them with love. God is love. Understanding how much you are loved is the key to showing love. Jesus loved us to the cross. Becoming a Christian means we are becoming love. To display the characteristics of Jesus means we must display and teach with love. Even when God chastises us, He does it in love. If you remember that, every message you prepare will be just what we need. How does the third Sunday in December sound to you?"

I look around the room as if considering my reply.

"If you need more time, we can look at another date," he says.

I shake my head, no. My mind is processing my response. It's best to get it over with. I have a little over a month to pray and prepare. That's enough time. I have prepared Bible Study lessons in a few days. I can do this. He sees I'm still thinking so he continues.

"This will give you a month or so to prepare. I don't want you to spend your holiday season consumed with this. That first sermon can be a little overwhelming on the nerves."

"You have a good point," I tell him.

"Besides, it is the Sunday before we have our Christmas festivities. Everyone will be so excited; you could get up there and say about anything and they will 'amen' to it."

I smile at his attempt to joke. He does have a point. Right before Christmas is a good time.

"Keep in mind, I'll be right here to help you in any way you need. All you have to do is ask and it's yours."

He gives me that perusing look I have almost become accustomed to. Almost. I get the feeling he's talking about more than sermon tips. I give a nod to show him I accept the date. I began mentally preparing myself to stand in front of the congregation. He continues to face me with an, I have more to say, but I'm not sure how to say it look on his face.

"Now to address the other matter." He pauses before he continues.

I feel my heart rate pick up. Is he about to talk about us? Is he interested in me? Is he about to tell me he is not? Did he see my reaction when his ex-mother-in-law said he was watching me? My mind is racing. He is struggling for words as hard as I am struggling to keep my composure. I soften my stare to try and make his next words easier. He manages to continue.

"This is harder than I remember it being. I don't remember having trouble talking to a woman."

I laugh in disbelief. "You have trouble talking to women?"

"What?" he says with a shy smile. "I'm out of practice. It's been a while since I tried to talk to a woman; since I've wanted to talk to a woman." His expression grows serious.

My body tenses up. He notices.

"I know you heard my mother-in-law's words. I'm sorry. I tried to not be so obvious, but I couldn't help myself. You are an amazing woman. I'm sorry. I don't mean to pressure you. I've had five years to cope with being single. You have only had a few months and the hounds are already after you."

He looks down again to prepare his next words. I can see he is struggling; I'm just not sure what to say. He continues.

"I've heard so many confessions of marriages starting for the wrong reasons and seen so many people in unhappy marriages. I decided if I couldn't convince Sherrie to stay married to me, I would simply stay single or wait until God sent the right one my way. It's easier for me to pray through temptations than pray through a bad marriage."

I remain silent. I understand that. Flashes of Richard goes through my head. Do I want a repeat of that? Pastor Collins is nothing like Richard. I feel warm and safe when he's around. It's like he is prepared to do anything to make my situation better. Although, he is this way around everyone. With Richard, I always felt I needed to watch what I did or said to not offend him. And when I did speak up, he always found a way to shut me down. He wanted us distanced in every way. And he succeeded.

"Michelle, this presented itself sooner than I wanted," Pastor continues. "But I want the chance to get to know you and you to know me. I can wait as long as you want me to. Don't think I'm rushing you. I just felt I needed to say something to explain myself."

He pauses and looks at me. I'm still speechless. I'm trying to form the words, but they won't come out of my mouth. I am interested. What woman wouldn't be? Well, Sherrie wasn't. I just don't want to rush into anything.

He begins to talk again. "If you're not interested, I understand."

I reach over and place my hand over his. He shivers at my touch but leaves his hand beneath mine.

"I think you are an amazing man Pastor Collins," I start.

"But." He stops my sentence and looks at my hand on his.

I pause and wait until his eyes come back up to meet mine. I smile. I do need more time, but there is no way I am letting this man get away from me without at least getting to know him. The real him. His eyes rest in mine. I feel him relax.

"As I was saying, I think you are an amazing man Pastor Collins. I would like time to get through my first sermon and then I would like to invite you over for dinner."

He stands and pulls me into an embrace.

"That sounds great. You won't regret it," he says.

After the initial shock of his instant move, I return his embrace. I pull away and look up at him.

"I do want to take things slow. I want to be sure this time."

He smiles. "Take all the time you need. Just to know you're willing to try is all I need. I'll take care of the rest."

He pulls me into another embrace. "Now let's get you ready for that sermon."

His hug does not feel inappropriate. I feel appreciated, admired, warm, safe. I feel loved.

Chapter 13

Over the next week, the pastor's words run through my mind. Becoming love. We are becoming love. As I interact with my co-workers at Harthwell's, I contemplate my actions. Am I showing love? Can they see God through me? One of my goals is to intermingle more with them, but some days it is not easy. Did I speak with love? Did I react in love? Some people in that office makes it hard to love them. Some days it's easier to simply avoid them. I speak and move on.

There are days I'm glad I have them to hang out with. Last Thursday someone stole Henry's lunch. Henry works in our IT department but loves to eat lunch with my co-workers. I think he is sweet on Susanne, but I never bothered to asks. We were all sitting at the lunch table watching him walk up and down the lunch container wall looking for his lunch. He became infuriated. He didn't see it. The more he walked, the antsier he became. He came back to the table with language that made me remember why I sat alone so much. When he angrily said, "somebody stole my pork chop sandwich." I almost fell of out my seat laughing. The whole table laughed.

"Who would steal another person's pork chop sandwich?" he barked. The more he complained. The harder we laughed. I tried to stop but couldn't. The more I laughed, the more everyone else laughed.

Soon Henry joined in. After we all settled down, the table chipped in and bought lunch for Henry.

"It's not my fried pork chop sandwich, but it will have to do." We all cracked up again.

Now to this sermon. There is so much to choose from. How do I approach this congregation in love? I prayed. Pastor said God would give me something to preach, but He has not spoken yet. It has already been a week and I have no idea what I am going to preach about. What is God waiting on? I need to prepare. I have looked over several of my old Bible Study lessons, but neither of them feels appropriate for a first sermon. I begin looking through Sunday School books for ideas. Is this what the pastor goes through every Sunday? He makes it seem so easy. Do I preach from the Old Testament or the New? Since my call into the ministry, I have watched Pastor Collin's technique and alignment of his sermons and how he opens and closes a sermon. He does it so gracefully. Even when his messages are correcting and instructing, they are delivered in love.

I close my Bible and go into the kitchen. Supper is so easy now that I can choose what I want to eat. I'm not hungry but it's already close to seven PM. I haven't eaten since lunch at work. I warm up some leftover vegetable soup and go to the table. My mind wanders back to my sermon. How can I prepare when I don't know what I'm preparing for?

"Trust God." He has proven Himself to me over and over, so why should this be any different. I exhale and begin my soup. I need to take my mind off this. God will provide, He always does. I can finish reading my book, 'Over the Top' by Drucilla Park. That's what I can do. I want to know if Dexter is going to quit his job and follow his wife to her promotion in Australia or let her go without him. Or, I could go for a walk before dark and then read. Yes. That sounds better.

"Becoming Love." The pastor's words ring in my spirit again. We are becoming love as we become like Christ. Is this what God wants my sermon to be. I go to my desk and open my Bible. My reading the night before was from Roman chapter twelve and it talked about how we are to love and treat others. I read the chapter. As I read, scripture content goes through my head. I smile. This is what God wants me to share with the congregation. If we are becoming like Christ, then we are becoming love. Relaxed, I look out of the window. It's not dark. I decide to go for a short walk to meditate on what God is showing me.

The remainder of my week is filled with scriptures and Bible passages run through my mind constantly. I decide to wait till after Sunday morning service to begin writing out my sermon. I want to get through Sunday School class before I begin. I'm glad I did. One of Pastor's encouraging pointers that morning was to give God time to speak. He says if we listen, God will guide us in the right direction.

I have quotes and Bible references scribbled on several note pads. Pastor also teaches us to study the who, what, when, where and why of a scripture passage to help understand what the Bible is trying to tell us. I am anxious to get to my sermon preparation. I can't wait to get home and start organizing it all.

With Sunday School class over, I rush to Pastor Collins' office. He always goes to his office in case someone needs to see him before service. I must admit, a part of me just wants to be alone with him. He has left me alone to prepare my sermon. I get the same loving greeting he gives all the members. I have caught him looking at me a couple of times. Once, we made eye contact and he winked at me. I know I blushed. I hope he didn't see it.

I remember a book on his shelf entitled "Love Beyond Love." It caught my eye months ago and I wanted to borrow it but forgot to ask. I remembered it this morning and can't think of a more appropriate time to read it. As I reach to knock, his door opens. Rev. Jones walks out. He pauses. He has an angry expression on his face. I guess I startled him. He has not spoken to me since the announcement of my call into the ministry.

"Hello, Reverend." I speak but he does not reply.

He brushes past me before I can stand back to give him a clear path. I step into the office. Pastor Collins looks agitated. I get the feeling that had something to do with me.

"Is this a good time?" I ask.

He tries to soften his expression. "Come on in, Michelle." He walks around his desk. His smile returns.

"Is everything all right?" I ask him.

"Nothing for you to worry about." He shifts his eyes from me as he says this.

"If it had something to do with me, it is."

He steps closer to me but stops before getting within arms reach. "You focus on getting ready for your trial sermon and let me worry about everyone else."

I can see he is trying to protect me, but I want to know what's going on, especially if it concerns me.

"Reverend Jones objects to me preaching here, doesn't he?" I ask.

"That's a nice way of putting it," he replies. "He is threatening to leave the church if I allow you in the pulpit."

"Whoa." I gasp. "I'm sorry I put you in that position. I don't have to get up there. We don't need all this confusion in the church."

He steps closer and looks down at me. Now he is close enough for me to reach out and touch him. "God called you and I agree with His call. As I stated earlier, you focus on your sermon and let me take care of the rest."

I want to wrap my arms around him but close my fist to keep my hands to myself. "What are you going to do?"

"I don't have to do anything." He smiles at me. "You have a sermon to preach and Rev. Jones can do what he chooses. I am simply waiting for a Word from the Lord." He gives me an assuring smile. "Now, was there a reason you came to my office or did you just want to be alone with me?"

I blush and stepped away from him. I get caught up in those golden eyes so easily. I forgot why I came to his office. I close my eyes to quickly clear my head.

"I come to borrow a book," I manage to get out.

"Oh, which one?" he asked.

"I remember seeing a book called 'Love Beyond Love' on your shelf. Do you still have it?"

"Yes, by Melinda Manifold. That's a good read. It was actually one of Sherri's and she recommended I read it."

I notice he pauses and averts his eyes when he says her name. I give him a reassuring smile. I understand we all have a past, but we also have a future.

He points to the tall bookshelf covering most of the wall in front of his desk. "Help yourself."

This man loves his book. There must be five hundred books in this office. I would love to see what he keeps at home. I walk to the bookshelf and start searching. I finally find it and of course, it is on the top shelf. I get on my tiptoes to reach it. I freeze when I feel someone reach over me. Unaware that he had walked over, I pause afraid to turn around. He is standing close enough for me to feel his clothes brush against me. I quickly compose myself and turn. He does not step back.

"Is this what you're looking for?" He looks down at me with that mesmerizing smile.

I forget to breathe. "Thank you. I'll return this as soon as I finish."

"Keep it. It's a girlie book anyway," he teases. "She does bring out some interesting points about love."

He stares at me when he says the last word. I freeze again. This man is going to drive me crazy. I turn my head to break his gaze.

"Thank you," I say and walk towards the door.

"Is this for your sermon?" he asks.

"Yes," I reply.

"What's your subject?"

"You will have to wait like everyone else." I smile.

"Well, I guess it has something to do with love." He stares at me with that smile again.

I shyly open the door. "See you in service."

I walk out of his office. How can he have that effect on me already? I can only imagine what it will be like to get to know him. Sermon Michelle. Focus. But he is so dreamy. I smile at my thoughts. We'll see what happens.

* * *

The church is almost full when I enter the sanctuary. I see several pairs of eyes watching me as I take my seat. I guess they have as much anticipation about my upcoming sermon as I do. Praise service is inspiring. I'm on my feet through the entire song selections.

When the deacons call for offering, I stand ready to walk around long before they get to my side of the congregation. Waiting to walk around the offering table, I see Angela walk up the aisle to give an offering. I feel a pounding in my chest. I almost fall back into my seat but catch myself on the seat in front of me. I have not seen or spoken to

Angela in almost four months since she and my husband walked out of my house together. She looks straight ahead. My breathing increases. A flood of emotions run through me. I get angry. I force myself to look down and not stare at her. I began to pray. I knew this day would come. I would eventually have to face her. I inhale, then exhale. She deserves to be in church. We all need to be in church.

"Father help me to be the example you have called me to be," I pray. "Jesus, I need You. Give me strength to love the way You would love. Guide my actions and my words to represent the calling you have placed on my life. In Your precious name I pray, Jesus. Amen."

I open my eyes to see Pastor Collins focused on me. He has a concerned but reassuring smile on his face. I give him a small nod to let him know I'm OK. I feel a wave of peace come over me. I give my offering and sit with a variety of scenarios running through my head. I notice Angela sitting on the last row. What if she wants to talk to me? I settle my thoughts. Maybe she just wants to be in the church like the rest of us. She came regularly before all that happened with Richard.

I begin to think of all the medical problems she has been facing. My heart becomes heavy. She and I have faced so much over the years. I can't help but wonder how she is doing. How did her surgery go? Was she still dealing with her headaches? I didn't get a good look at her to see if she looks better or worse.

"Bless and watch over her Jesus." Without thinking, I feel myself praying for her wellbeing. She and Richard are in my past. I don't hate Angela. For some reason, I feel sorry for her. I get the feeling she was as caught up in Richard's grasp as I was. Maybe someday, in the far future, I will get the opportunity to talk with her. I don't know if I'm ready yet.

Pastor's sermon is uplifting. 'I Can,' with the scripture reference of Philippians chapter four, verse thirteen. 'I can do all things through Christ which strengtheneth me.' A simple message but delivered with the powerful assurance that we should believe in ourselves because of the Christ that is within us.

Pastor declares, "the Apostle Paul states in the passages before our scripture text that he has learned to be content in whatever state he is in. He has learned to live humble and to live in prosperity; to suffer through having plenty and having nothing. If you notice, he says he has learned, through Christ to trust in himself. I walk in confidence because I've learned to trust the Christ within me. I learned to hold my head high because Christ is with me. If we learn to believe in who we are in Christ, all things are possible. Christ wants to work through us, but we must believe He can."

As he preaches, I feel my confidence strengthens. I must stand up there in a couple of weeks and face this same audience. I can do this. I encourage myself. People don't have to like it or agree with it. They didn't call me, God did. And I must do what He called me to do.

I feel ready when Pastor calls for the benediction. I stand. Sermon notes are running rapidly through my mind. I even jotted down a few more as Pastor was preaching. I'm eager to get home and work on my sermon. I am stopped by several members for hugs and well wishes as I head to Pastor Collins for my final hug of the day. I plan to commend him on another great sermon and head home to prepare. He has a line waiting to greet him, so it takes me a few minutes to get there. He is as polite as always and sends me on my way.

Most of the congregation has left when I step out of the church. When I make it to the bottom of the steps and look around to my car, someone is standing at my driver's door.

Angela.

Chapter 14

I freeze when we make eye contact. Why is she standing near my car? Rage runs through me. My mind starts yelling ugly remarks to say to her. How dare she. It takes me a minute to get my feet to move forward. When they do move, it's at a slower than normal pace. I never take my eyes away from hers. She looks at the ground then back up at me. I try to read her expression, but all I see is sadness. I feel my heart soften. It's hard to be angry at her when she appears to be in so much pain. She is in your past, Michelle. I finally reach my car. I see her inhale and release a long breath. I guess she is as nervous about this interaction as I am; maybe more than I am.

I stop about five feet in front of her. I want to get home and work on my sermon, but I convince myself to be polite as possible and hear what she has to say. I don't know what it is she could have to say to me, but I prepare myself to listen. God has been working on me for months about forgiveness. I heard a preacher once say, "forgiveness is remembering without the pain." I remember all too well what she and Richard put me through and, the pain is almost gone. Well, it was. I'm not quite ready to face her. I guess it's time to get ready.

"Hello, Michelle." Angela looks and me then back at the ground.

"Angela," I say very drily. I pause. I'm trying hard to fight the feeling brewing inside me. The feeling to unleash pinned up frustration. My words and demeanor could easily make this conversation proceed good or bad. I can tell by the way she's looking; she's not here to hurt me. I honestly don't know what she could say or do to hurt me more than she already has. She looks as if she wants to cry.

"Michelle, I wanted to see, uh, can I talk to you?" she stumbles over her words.

I can see this is hard for her. I try and keep a pleasant look on my face. It's not easy. A part of me wants to hear what she has to say, and the other part wants to tell her off and drive away. My sermon title goes through my mind. Becoming Love. Of course, God would step in at a time like this. Sometimes I wish He would leave me to show my true colors. But then I always thank Him for stepping in to show how wonderful He is. Now is one of those times.

"I don't want to talk out here," she says. "People are staring at us. Can I take you to lunch? I owe you an explanation and a huge apology. Please give me the chance to explain."

I'm almost afraid to hear what she has to say. I just got to where I could function without the pain of my husband walking out on me with my best friend, and now she wants to bring it all back up again. She can tell I'm contemplating my answer.

"Please, Michelle. I am sorry. It was not as it looked and I want to explain," she says.

Pain and rage go through me. My mouth opens.

"You, my best friend, tells me you're pregnant by my husband," I bark. "How is that supposed to look?" *Calm down Michelle*, I tell myself.

"Please Michelle, let me explain." Tears form in her eyes. "I'm so sorry."

I see people standing at their cars looking our way. The parking lot is half empty and many want to see how this plays out.

"Where do you want to go for lunch?" I ask her. I want to get away from here as much as she does.

"We can go wherever you want to go," she says.

"I was going to Bruce's and grab some lunch to take home. But, too many people from church go there on Sunday."

"You're right," she says. "We can go to Mitchell's Deli. They are small but have very good food. My treat." She gives me a pleading look.

"That's fine," I say. "I'll meet you there." I know I sound dry and uncaring, but I am trying to be polite. This meeting is as difficult as I imagined it would be. So many things have built up in my head to say to Angela. Now I have the opportunity, I don't want to bother. I just want to move past that phase in my life. What will I accomplish by saying things to make her feel bad only to feel awful later for saying them?

She looks at me with genuine gratitude. "Thank you."

We go to our separate cars for the drive to Mitchell's. I pray along the way. The theme of my message continues to run through my head; 'Becoming Love.' If I am to preach about love, I must show it.

"Jesus, I need you to help me through this. I am trying, but I'm only flesh. Show me what You would do in this situation. Allow me to show Your love." I feel better after I pray. A little.

As soon as we sit in the restaurant, the waitress comes to our table. I order the house salad. I do not have an appetite anymore, but I didn't want to appear rude. Angela appears to have built up her nerves. She begins the conversation.

"I hear you are about to give your first sermon."

I nod. My mind is not on the intricacies of standing in front of a congregation, but now that she has mentioned it, I would like to get home and work on my sermon. She continues.

"I am so excited. I wanted to call you and congratulate you, but I was afraid."

Her excitement fades. She looks at me then at the table.

"Michelle, I'm sorry. I wanted to tell you long ago. I tried to tell you so many times, but you were so crazy about Richard and I didn't want to take your happiness."

"So, you decide to sleep with him?" I ask trying to keep my feelings at bay.

"It's not like that, Michelle. Honestly. I never meant to hurt you. I tried to get away from him. He just has this way of getting what he wants."

I give her a questioned look. This is Angela. She has had men wrapped around her little finger since high school.

"Let me go back," she says.

"Richard and I started messing around when you and I were in the tenth grade. He was a senior and dating Regina, the cheerleading captain. You remember Regina, the girl who looked she belonged on the Dallas Cowboys Cheerleading Squad. He told me I could not tell anyone. He said he didn't want her but had to be with her because the football captain should be with the cheerleading captain. Me being young and stupid believed him and keep my mouth shut. Even from you. It was never anything serious. He only came around when he wanted company. I should have told you then and this would have never happened.

"After high school, I realized how easy it was to get what I wanted from men. You went off to college and I stayed here and did what comes naturally for me. When Richard found out he was not the only one, he tried to get me to let the others go but I wouldn't. He didn't make enough money to tell me who I could or could not see, but he was good at." Her words trail off.

She stops before finishing her sentence. She knows I'm aware of what Richard is good at.

"He and I never got serious. To me, he was like every other man; wanting women stashed on every corner to stop by at their convenience. He only came by every couple of months, so I knew he was seeing someone else. When you returned from college, it took us a while to reconnect. When we did, you were head over hills for him. Soon after, you announced your engagement. It all happened so fast. I tried to talk you out of it. You remember, I told you to wait. Make sure he was going to be faithful."

I do remember her trying several times to talk me out of marrying Richard. I guess it's not her fault, I was in love. But she could have just told me she was sleeping with him.

"I knew he didn't love you, but you were so happy. Every time I tried to match you with someone in school, it turned into a disaster. I had never seen you as happy as you were with him. My plan was to leave him alone and hope he treats you right. You were a good person. You have always been, and you deserved to be treated right."

The waitress brings our food. Angela looks at me. I have a blank expression. I can't say anything. I am processing all she is saying. It all aligns with what I know to be true. I believe her. I still can't understand how she ended up in my house walking out with my husband. She waits for the waitress to walk away and continue.

"He came to see me the night before your wedding. We argued. I explained to him that you were my best friend. My only real friend. He insisted it would be the last time. I tried to resist, but Richard can be so persuasive."

She looked down at the fries on her plate. She rolls one around in the ketchup then looks back at me. I still can't find any words to express how I feel. I'm not sure I want to know all of this, but she looks as if she needs to get it off her chest.

"I'm sorry Michelle. I have rehearsed this moment in my head so many times. I promised myself if I could ever get you to talk to me again, I would tell you everything. You were such a good friend and I messed that up. I know we can never be that way again, but I can't live with myself knowing how much I hurt you and have you hate me."

"I don't hate you Angela. It is hard for me to understand how you ended up in my bedroom though."

"I'm getting to that. I have no excuse. I wanted you to know it was not done on purpose and I never planned to hurt you, especially the way he did. The way we did.

"I felt awful at your wedding. Him standing there smiling at you. I told myself, at least it's over. Later in your marriage, I could tell from the stories you told me, he was just using you for the money, but you seemed to be happy. He stayed away from me for about five years. Then one day, he just shows up on my doorstep. I would not let him in my apartment. He tried a couple more times over the next few years, but I never gave him a chance.

"As you got deeper in church, I saw more of him in the streets and everywhere else. You and I also seemed to spend less time together. You were serious about God and I only went to church to look at the Pastor and see who else would catch my eye. Several of my male friends are there every Sunday.

"Then, one day I went to the mall to meet up with someone. I don't remember who it was. I was sitting in the food court and one of my migraines hit. I sat there almost in tears my head hurt so badly. Richard walks up. He was with someone but brushes her off to come to my rescue. I dug my medicine out of my purse, but it takes about thirty minutes for it to take effect. He offered to drive me home. My head hurt so bad, I just wanted to get out of there.

"By the time my head calmed down, I realized we are in my bedroom, sitting on the side of my bed. I saw the way he looked at me and got up off the bed. He began his lines about how bad your marriage was. He assured me it was over, and he was just looking for the right time to leave. My mind didn't want to, but the rest of me gave in. You and I only talked every few months, so I was not sure what was going on. When we did talk, you mostly complained about him so I figured you would divorce him soon.

"Honestly Michelle, I didn't want Richard, he was just a good time. He was simply another one of my men. Part of me liked using him because he was using you. I took his money, which I later found out was your money. That made me feel worse. I listened to his lies about what he wanted to do for me. I had no intention of sharing a life with Richard. If he cheated on you, I knew he would cheat on me and I would definitely cheat on him. I have never had the mindset to settle down with one man, you know that.

"A few months before the incident at your house, my migraines become worse and lasted longer periods of time. Then the stomach pains appeared. I was going to my doctor more often and of course; I couldn't see my gentlemen friends as often as I liked. I depended on your friendship more. You always prayed for me. Richard called frequently. I figured he was just bored. I was too, so I talked to him. Listening to both of you, I knew neither of you was happy in your marriage, but after all this time, I couldn't say anything even if I wanted to.

When the doctor finally realized I was pregnant and that was causing my added problems, Richard flipped. He said he had always wanted a son but didn't want one with you."

A jolt of pain runs through me as I remember his words. I remain silent and let her finish.

"He said this was his chance to get out and he was leaving you. I was scared and did not want to go through this alone. He insisted on going with me. From the way the both of you had been talking, I assumed your marriage had been over. He called me over that morning to pick him up for the airport. He said he broke things off with you that morning and you would not be there when I arrived.

"Michelle, I know what I did was wrong, but I honestly never meant to hurt you. The way Richard talked to you that morning tore my heart out."

Tears run down her cheek. The thought of his words fills my eyes with tears.

"I could not believe he said those things to you. It was bad enough that your husband and best friend had been caught, but to have him degrade you in that way. I was too embarrassed to say anything, but I knew then I was done with Richard. Any man who can say those things to a woman is beneath even me. We did wrong, not you. Yet he talked to you like you had done something wrong. I barely spoke to him on the trip.

"When the doctor in Indiana couldn't do anything to save the baby, I had to come home and have the surgery to remove it. Richard stayed with me for three weeks until I recovered enough to get around my place without assistance. He slept in my guest bedroom. Then I made him get out. I made it clear it was over between us and how much I disapproved of the way he talked to you.

"No words can explain how bad I feel about messing up our friendship over a sorry man like Richard. He did not deserve you. He does not even deserve me and I'm not worth anything. I just want you to know I was not deceitfully grinning in your face and sneaking around, not the way it seemed. I am just another silly weak woman who needs to get her life together. I have spent a lot of time thinking about my future lately. I am truly sorry and hope one day you can forgive me."

She looks at me with tears still running down her face. I have used a tissue to wipe my tears several times.

"I forgive you, Angela. And I believe you. Everything you say aligns with what I already know to be true. Yes, you hurt me, but God is helping me to move on. He can work wonders in our lives if we let Him."

I give her an assuring smile to let her know I mean what I say.

"Thank you for giving me the chance to explain. I know I messed up," she says. "But maybe in time, we will be able to go to lunch every now and then. I really miss you, and I messed up when I needed you most. That surgery almost killed me, and I only had Richard and my sister to help. I think she only came by to see if I would make it."

I smile. Still Angela.

"Maybe in time," I reply. I feel like the less I say at this point the better.

"Would it be OK if I come to hear you preach? Everyone is excited. You are all they're talking about. I know I don't have to ask to come to church, but if you don't want me there, I will stay at home."

"I would love it if you came, Angela."

She smiles and wipes her tears. I eat my salad and politely smile as she rambles on about her medical struggles and relationships. She reassures me that she is done with Richard. She says he is living with one of his ex-girlfriends across town.

I don't know what, if anything, will come of our relationship. We have a long way to go, but we are off to a decent start. I have forgiven Angela. I pray the best for her. I even feel a sense of relief knowing she is the person I have known since grade school. A woman, like the rest of us, who has made some mistakes and needs God to help get back on the right path.

Chapter 15

I awaken early on the third Sunday morning of December. My night was restless. The anticipation of my first sermon caused excitement and my nerves to run wild much of the night. I have listened to God, prayed and prepared. I can do this. Pastor Collins calls me the night before my sermon to check on me.

"Excited?" he asks.

"That and a couple of other emotions I can't quite describe," I reply.

I hear him chuckle. "You're ready for this. I don't know anyone more qualified to be used by God. Just relax and trust Him. Remember, those He calls, He qualifies. He chose you as a vessel to use. Allow Him to use you."

"I hear you Pastor. I'm ready. I have prayed and studied. He did tell me to study to show myself approved. It was not as bad as I thought. Scriptures and references came to me from all over the place. I just had to find the actual verses, study background and put it all together. Standing in front of a crowd and delivering it is a different story."

"You'll do fine. You stand confidently in front of the congregation all the time," he says.

"I know, but this is not the same. Too many people don't want me there, in that pulpit."

"What did I tell you about that," he says. "You focus on the message and let me take care of the rest. Besides, we must get through this. I have a dinner waiting on me." He paused.

I remained silent. I've spent the last month trying, unsuccessfully most of the time, to push him out of my mind.

"You did not forget my dinner, did you?" he asked me.

"No," I replied. "It's just hard to concentrate on my studies when I think of you."

I hear his voice lighten up. "Well, as I said, all the more reason to get through this sermon."

"Easier said than done," I said.

He laughed again. Then, his laughter quietened. "Remember, we are all here to support you and most importantly, to hear a word from the Lord. Something I learned long ago, never waste an opportunity God gives to share His Word. You may feel you are in the spotlight, but what people need to see and hear is God. So again, relax and allow Him to use you."

"I will Pastor and thank you for calling to check on me."

"You're welcome. Now get some rest. Good night Michelle."

"Good night Pastor."

As the phone went silent, I thought, 'what will I call him if I date him or even become his wife?'

I tried to push the image of him out of my mind. I needed rest. It didn't work. Between thoughts of my sermon and him, I barely slept four hours last night.

Now here I sit at my table with a cup of coffee reading over my sermon again. Tired of sitting in the house alone, I dress and head to the church. I arrive only thirty minutes before Sunday School, so I don't feel too bad. Pastor Collins and one of the deacons are the only cars on the lot. I decide not to let Pastor know I have arrived. He is in my head enough already. Members will start arriving soon. I just need to hang out in the back for a few minutes and then head to the sanctuary.

I walk to my Sunday School classroom. A quiet, empty place to hide. I sit at the large oval table in the middle of the room. The kids? I have not given much thought to what I will do after I became a minister. Pastor Collins told me I would sit in the pulpit with the other ministers after my first sermon. But, what about teaching the kids. I love teaching the kids Sunday School and Bible Study classes. I see no reason to quit. I will discuss it with Pastor. I don't think he will object. I will be in the sanctuary for every service.

So much is about to change. Sitting up front looking out into the congregation will be much different from sitting in the congregation looking up at four or five persons in the pulpit. Now there will be around five-hundred pairs of eyes constantly staring at me. Every movement, every gesture will be seen by someone or everyone. People notice everything. The way you dress, fix your hair even the accessories you wear to compliment your wardrobe will be scrutinized. Not to mention if I get sleepy. I am about to be put in a spotlight. A big spotlight.

I have always tried to monitor my actions and words. I learned early in my walk with Christ that people are always looking for a reason to reject Christ, and Christians usually give them that reason. I have heard on several occasions, "if saved people live like that, I don't need to be saved. They do the same things I do and I don't claim to be a Christian." Some people will use any excuse to get out of going to church and learning more about what God expects of us.

Now, I will be in a spotlight more than ever. I guess that's all a part of the call. Pastor says we are called to a lifestyle as much as we are called to preach God's Word. This train of thought is not helping to calm my nerves. I get up and walk to the sanctuary to await the women's Sunday School class. There should be a couple of ladies in by now.

Sunday School is uneventful. I am greeted by most of the ladies as they come in. This is good. Most of them seem to be in good spirits. Several watch me and whisper throughout the whole class. The first female preacher in our church is big news. Their support is invaluable. Pastor sends one of the ushers instructing me to come to his office after Sunday School. He is sitting on the corner of his desk when I enter.

"How are you feeling?" he asks.

"I've had better mornings." His smile puts me at ease.

He walks over to me, throws his arm over my shoulder and pulls me close for a hug.

"You got this," he smiles down at me.

There goes my resolve. I melt. He sees my reaction and laughs.

"Have a seat." He walks around his desk still giggling at me.

"What is so funny?" I ask him.

"Nothing. If you only could see what I see. I'm just happy. God is about to do something amazing through this ministry and you are a big part of it."

"Do you mind letting me in on the secret?" I ask.

"Later. Today I want you to focus on allowing God to use you. Do you want some time alone to pray or get your thoughts together?"

"No. I am as ready as I'm going to get. I would like for you to pray with me before I go into the sanctuary."

"Now that I will be more than happy to do. Did you get a good night's rest?"

"Not really," I say.

He smiles again. "That's normal. This is a big day."

He proceeds to make small talk. I think he's trying to calm my nerves. It works, a little. He manages to get me to laugh at a couple of his jokes. They temporarily take my mind off what is ahead of me. Then he stands and walks around his desk.

"Ready to pray and go in?" he asks.

I nod. He reaches over and takes both my hands into his. My heart rate increases. This is it. I try to calm my nerves. I silently pray as I prepare for him to start. He looks down at me until I make eye contact. I finally look up to meet his gaze.

"God's got this." That smile puts me at ease. I feel my muscles relax as I bow my head. He begins to pray.

"Lord God, we thank You for all You are to us. You continue to watch over us individually and as a church family. Your blessings are beyond measure. You have brought us to some unimaginable task and then You brought us through those same tasks. You have proven Yourself many times over and for this we trust You.

"Now Lord, come into Your house this morning and show Yourself mighty. Move Minister Michelle out of the way and allow Your Spirit to flow through her. Give her the peace of mind to know that You called her because You know she is a willing vessel ready for Your use. Send a Word to Your people this morning to show You are still in control. Open our hearts and minds to receive the message and the messenger. We look to You Jesus who is the author and the finisher of our faith. It is in Your precious and mighty name we pray Jesus. Amen."

"Amen, and thank you Pastor."

"You ready to go in?" he asks me.

"This is it."

He smiles, steps to the side and points at the door for me to lead the way.

When we enter, the sanctuary is packed, and people are still coming through the door. My mind freezes. My eyes glaze over and I must remind myself to breathe. Pastor Collins points for me to enter the pulpit and take the seat directly behind the podium. Reverend Lewis and Reverend McCormick greets me in the pulpit with a smile and embrace. There are three other male ministers sitting in the pulpit. I don't recognize them. They greet me with a warm welcome. I guess they are here out of curiosity or to support Pastor Collins. I am grateful to be accepted by them. Pastor walks over and enthusiastically greets them as if they are life-long friends. I smile at their transaction.

I don't see Reverend Jones. He did say he would not share the pulpit with a woman. That is his choice. He is accountable to God, not me. I prepared myself for rejection from some today while trusting God to shine through with a message to be accepted by others. Some may say I'm wrong for being in the pulpit, but the Word of God is right, I don't care whose mouth it comes out of.

I take my seat. This is good. I'm short and hid behind the podium from most of the congregation. I have time to pray and compose myself. God is good. He is mighty. He is worthy to be praised. If He says I can, then who's to say I can't. He is more than the world against me. I feel His Spirit strengthening inside me. God is here. God is with me.

"Thank you, Jesus. I need you and I love you."

Pastor Collins stands to the podium and opens service. I stand and look out over the still growing audience. I am amazed. I guess this is a big deal for our church. I recognize many of the faces I see. My parents came. My dad even came in the church with my mother this time. My heart warms. I hope they will go out to lunch with me afterward. I notice Angela in the crowd of people. Exhaling, I scan the congregation in admiration.

I look to the right and see Reverend Jones sitting on the front row with several other men dressed in suits looking tailor-made. Deacon Green is sitting off to the side of them. I examine them for a minute, but neither of them will make eye contact with me. I guess their job is to be intimidating. It's not working. I have prayed and prepared for this. I serve a powerful God. If I am nervous, it's because I want to be sure I'm not misleading God's people. I want to represent God well. Every word will be scrutinized by someone. So, there is no need to try and please man, but please God. I clear my head and focus.

"Let this be You, God." I pray.

Pastor looks to the right at the gentlemen on the front row. "I am glad to see the district elders representing today."

When he says this, I feel a slight wave of panic run over me. He calls each by name and extended an invitation for them to join us in the pulpit. Four of the men look at the one sitting furthest to the right. He holds up his hand and declines the offer. The others follow his gesture. I feel a sense of relief. I look down at my hands. My fingers are intertwined. I feel my heart rate increase. Then I feel a soothing cloud encompass me. I exhale. This is God. I recognize it from other times He has come to my rescue. I smile. Unfold my hands. Hold my head up and prepare to worship my God. He is my joy. He is my strength. He is everything I need. And He is here with me, right now. Thank you, Father.

Pastor proceeds to thank each of the ministers in the pulpit, calling each by name. Church service goes through the normal Sunday morning routine covering praise and worship, choir selections, announcements and offering. I stand on my feet as in my usual praise several times determined not the let my inner jitters deter me from praising God. He has been too good to me.

Then the pastor stands to announce me. I lower my head and pray.

"Let this be You, God."

"New Jerusalem, we serve a mighty God. He has been so good to us over the years and I look forward to what He is about to do through this ministry. Today is an exciting day. I stand to bring to the front an amazing servant in the gospel, helper in the church and friend to many. She really needs no introduction to those of us who have had the pleasure of serving with her. She has served in the church for over fifteen years in many capacities. She is currently doing a great job as one of our youth instructors, but God has so much more in store for her."

He looks back at me and gives me that assuring smile. I hold his gaze and return a smile. He turns back to the audience.

"I know this is something new for our little church. We have never had a female minister stand behind the podium. Regardless of how we feel about it, God has called it into being. And I want my sister to know her pastor supports her calling one hundred percent. 'And I say unto you my friends, Be not afraid of them that kill the body, and after that have no more that they can do. But I will forewarn you whom ye shall fear: Fear him, which after he hath killed hath power to cast into hell; yea, I say unto you, Fear him.'"

I smile. He recites Luke chapter twelve verses four through five. I have read those scriptures several times since my calling. For him to recite them in front of the district leaders is even more assuring. I relax. God is with me and my pastor supports me. I simply need to stand and trust God.

"Without prolonging the time," Pastor Collins continues, "the next voice you hear after the choir is our very own Minister Michelle Hill."

He looks at me. "Minister Hill. Preach the Word."

It feels strange hearing my name preceded by the title 'Minister.' I pray as the choir sings 'All Hail King Jesus.' As they close the song, I stand to the podium. My heart rate increases uncontrollably. The church is silent. All eyes are on me.

"Let this be You, God." I silently pray.

Chapter 16

"Our God is an awesome God. I thank Him for the many blessings He has bestowed upon my life. I thank Him for seeing something in me that I could not see in myself. I honor Him for entrusting me to represent Him on this earth and praise Him for the strength to move beyond myself to obedience. He never promised me this walk would be easy, but He did promise to be with me every step of the way. Knowing this keeps me humble and grateful.

"To my pastor, I would not be standing here if not for you. I thank you for your guidance and support. You are a true example for many to follow. To the ministers present today, I thank you for your acceptance and support. To my New Jerusalem church family, know that I love you and I thank you. You have been very supportive since the announcement of my calling and I ask you all to keep me in your prayers.

"And now to share the message God has given me. Our scripture text will be coming from Romans chapter twelve verses nine and ten. The book of Romans chapter twelve verses nine and ten."

I slowly repeat my scripture to give everyone time to find it. I hear pages turning and look up to see many people standing awaiting me to continue. I began to read.

"Romans chapter twelve verses nine and ten from the King James Version reads, *Let* love be without dissimulation. Abhor that which is evil; cleave to that which is good. *Be* kindly affectioned one to another with brotherly love; in honour preferring one another;"

I look over the congregation as everyone takes their seat.

"Becoming Love." I pause and recite my subject again, "Becoming Love."

"In one of my discussions with Pastor Collins, he stated that as Christians, we are becoming love. In order to draw others to Christ, we must display Godly love and this kind of love can only come from a relationship with Jesus. The dictionary defines love as an intense feeling of deep affection or a great interest and pleasure in something. Listen to this, a strong or constant affection for and dedication to another."

I say these words again slowly, 'a strong or constant affection and dedication to another.'

"Our idea of love is generally centered around someone we are attached to physically or genetically connected to by our bloodlines. Our love is tied to our emotions and as our emotions shift, the level of love we display shifts. Basically, we love according to the way we feel. In physical relationships, we love as long as we are getting what we want in return. As long as you obey my rules, I love you. As long as you pay the bills, I love you. As long as you buy me what I want, I love you. As long as you fulfill my needs, I love you.

"But let that man stop handing out money or paying the bills. Let that woman stop sleeping in the same bed with you. Let that teenager refuse to follow your rules or become pregnant. Let that sibling not share the family inheritance or molest one of our children. That love goes out the window. Our type of love, the natural love, changes or sometimes altogether leaves according to the way we feel, or the way we are treated. It takes the inner workings of Jesus to overcome these situations and help us to continue in love. We may remember what the person did, or remember how they acted, but we can't allow it to hurt us to the point that we can't love past it.

"God's love for us is not subject to the way we act or treat Him. His love goes beyond what we do. His love represents who He is. He looks past our sinful flesh and sees what's inside us. We are His creation, carrying His breath of life in us. God loves His creation. John three, sixteen states, 'For God so loved the world, that he gave his only begotten Son, that whosoever believeth in him should not perish, but have everlasting life.' God loves us so much that He sent His Son, Jesus, to give everlasting life to those who believe. It is only through Jesus we can have this everlasting life."

I hear pastor in the background saying amen repeatedly. My voice has risen to another level. I feel the Spirit of God helping me. I look down at my notes. I have my sermon written out, but I have only looked down a few times. I continue.

"To understand the degree of His love, we must go to His word. His word shows His love goes beyond the way we treat Him. Romans five and eight states, 'But God commendeth his love toward us, in that, while we were yet sinners, Christ died for us.' This means while we were running the streets, doing everything we thought we were old enough to do, Jesus was allowing them to put nails in His hands and in His feet. While we were breaking up marriages, stealing jobs, trying every drug known to man and telling lies just to be telling lies, Jesus was hanging on the cross saying 'Father forgive them for they know not what they do.

"The kind of love we need cannot be found in books, cannot be learned in seminars, cannot be taught and definitely cannot be faked. The kind of love we need must come from inside and only Jesus can put it there. Now this love can be developed, but this development is built on the foundation of Jesus.

"During the time the Apostle Paul wrote the letter to the church at Rome, historians say about fifty-seven years after the death, burial and resurrection of Christ; the church was in disarray. Confessing Christ in some places meant exile from the community, imprisonment or even death. Yet the church at Rome was mostly Gentiles coming into the faith because the witness of Jesus was so powerful, people were drawn to it. Imagine being killed for just calling on the name of Jesus. People risked their lives, yet there was something about Jesus that drew them.

"In his letter, the Apostle Paul explains how the Gentiles are guilty before God; how the Jews are guilty before God and how the whole world is guilty before God. But, through faith in Jesus Christ, we are justified unto salvation. After he covers the basics of their salvation, which is the same basis we live by today, he explains the Christian struggle, death to sin and life in the Spirit.

"With the foundation of the Christian faith covered, by the time the Apostle Paul gets to chapter twelve, he is focused on the Christian conduct. He opens the chapter urging the church to present their bodies a living sacrifice, holy and acceptable unto God. He then tells them to be not conformed to this world, but to be transformed by the renewing of their minds, to prove that good, acceptable and perfect will of God. He is telling them to not remain conformed to the standards of the world, to not act like the conventional religious person of their day, but to be transformed into the image of Christ.

"Our sanctification is what sets us apart from the world. Where the world seeks status and power, we seek to show God has no respect of person. Where the world seeks material things, we seek the Spirit of God. Where the world seeks to hate, we must love. Love unconditional. Love in spite of. Love when we're treated right and love when we're treated wrong. Love when things are given and love when things are taken away. Love."

I hear 'that's right' and 'amen' coming from all over the congregation. As I speak, I look over the congregation, but I do not seem to focus on anyone. It's like God is using me to speak to everyone and no one person is singled out. I continue.

"Verses nine and ten of our scripture text says, "*Let* love be without dissimulation. Abhor that which is evil; cleave to that which is good. *Be* kindly affectioned one to another with brotherly love; in honour preferring one another. The Apostle Paul is teaching the Christians in Rome that their love should be sincere. They should hate that which is evil and cling to the good. Be devoted and respect one another. During a time when they risked imprisonment for their belief, they were taught to love their accusers and cling to each other for strength."

I walk away from the podium and look over the audience. With the microphone in my hand, I continue to speak. I notice Pastor is standing on his feet behind me, but I don't turn to look at him.

"We are not far from these standards today. People are hated because of their skin color or social status. Mistreated because of their nationality and downgraded because of their beliefs. As followers of Christ, we are called to be examples of His love. If the church does not show love, we cannot expect the world to show it."

I walk back to my Bible and flip to another passage I have marked for today's message. I read Matthew chapter five verses forty-three through forty-six.

"Matthew chapter five verses forty-three through forty-six says, Ye have heard that it hath been said, Thou shalt love thy neighbour, and hate thine enemy. But I say unto you, Love your enemies, bless them that curse you, do good to them that hate you, and pray for them which despitefully use you, and persecute you; That ye may be the children of your Father which is in heaven: for he maketh his sun to rise on the evil and on the good, and sendeth rain on the just and on the unjust. For if ye love them which love you, what reward have ye? do not even the publicans the same?"

I pause for a few seconds after reading the scripture.

"In our natural state, we find it impossible to love some people. Yet, Jesus commands us to love. Love our enemies. Those who curse us, lie on us, steal from us and mistreat us. Remember, if Jesus commands, He will provide what we need to make it come to pass.

"Melinda Manifold in her book 'Love Beyond Love' says that to love someone who has wronged us, we must learn to look beyond what the person has done. She says to do this, we should look within ourselves and find the worse thing about us. That weakness or sin that torments or hinders us from becoming the fullness of ourselves. The thing we think is hidden from everyone else. The thing we ask God to remove but He won't. We are to take that sin or weakness and place it on our worse enemy; on the person we find it hardest to love. Then we should realize that if God loves us with that fault, if Jesus died to cover that sin, we can give that same love to someone else. We all have sinned and fall short of His glory.

"I don't have to agree with you to love you. I don't have to like the things you do to love you. I don't have to follow you to love you. To love you, I must look past what you do and see who you are. You are my brother and my sister in Christ. You are my Father's creation, flaws included, same as I am."

To close my sermon, I flip my Bible to First Corinthians chapter thirteen and read the entire chapter.

"Though I speak with the tongues of men and of angels, and have not charity, I am become *as* sounding brass, or a tinkling cymbal.

And though I have *the gift of* prophecy, and understand all mysteries, and all knowledge; and though I have all faith, so that I could remove mountains, and have not charity, I am nothing.

And though I bestow all my goods to feed *the poor*, and though I give my body to be burned, and have not charity, it profiteth me nothing.

Charity suffereth long, *and* is kind; charity envieth not; charity vaunteth not itself, is not puffed up,

Doth not behave itself unseemly, seeketh not her own, is not easily provoked, thinketh no evil;

Rejoiceth not in iniquity, but rejoiceth in the truth;

Beareth all things, believeth all things, hopeth all things, endureth all things.

Charity never faileth: but whether *there be* prophecies, they shall fail; whether *there be* tongues, they shall cease; whether *there be* knowledge, it shall vanish away.

For we know in part, and we prophesy in part.

But when that which is perfect is come, then that which is in part shall be done away.

When I was a child, I spake as a child, I understood as a child, I thought as a child: but when I became a man, I put away childish things.

For now we see through a glass, darkly; but then face to face: now I know in part; but then shall I know even as also I am known.

And now abideth faith, hope, charity, these three; but the greatest of these *is* charity."

I walk away from the podium and face the congregation. Pacing the pulpit and I deliver my closing.

"Becoming love is the greatest accomplishment we can achieve as a Christian. To love others, we need to understand how much we are loved. The kind of love that looks beyond our faults to supply our needs. God knew we as a people need to be saved. From sin, from hatred, from jealously, from ourselves. Over two-thousand years ago He sent His Son, Jesus, to be that savior. He walked this earth, among sinners. He ate with sinners. He fellowshipped with sinners. He chose sinners to turn into disciples. He allowed sinners to mock and ridicule Him. He allowed sinners to take Him from judgment hall to judgment hall. He allowed sinners to put nails in His hands and nails in His feet. He allowed sinners to hang Him on a cross. He committed His life to the Father for sinners like you and me. He allowed sinners to lay Him in Joseph's borrowed tomb. But after three days, for the love of sinners, He got up. For sinners, He rose with all power in His hands. Today, He sits at the right hand of the Father and for sinners, He intercedes. Jesus, through His Holy Spirit, gives us His love. We can only show it to others if we become like Him. God is love. God gives love. God shows love. To love like Jesus, we must become love.

"The doors of the church are open."

* * *

I lay the microphone on the podium and turn for my seat. I step into Pastor Collin's arms. He holds me in a full embrace. The choir erupts with a rendition of 'Our God Is An Awesome God." A perfect song for the end of the day.

"Awesome," Pastor whispers in my ear. "No one could have delivered that message better. God has really used you."

He releases me and the other ministers in the pulpit are in line to embrace me. I notice almost the entire church is on their feet with cheers and applause. The district leaders slowly stand. I feel appreciated as my heart warms. Reverend Jones remains seated although he applauses without looking at me. I guess it's a matter of pride more than anything at this point. Once the choir finishes, I take my seat. Pastor Collins stands at the podium. The congregation quietens.

"God has shown up in this place today. God is love and we must become love if we want to be like Him. Minister Michelle, that was outstanding preaching. God really used you today. Anyone doubting God's ability to use a woman needs to hear that message. I don't know any man who could have delivered it better. I surely could not have."

The congregation applauds. He continues.

"I am truly full. That was a blessed Word and I will definitely be meditating on it all down the week. Anyone lacking fellowship with Jesus needs to come down and join their life to Him today. After that message, anyone doubting the love of God needs to come down today and renew their relationship with God. He is love and He loves each of us so much. It doesn't matter what we have done, God will restore us back into His loving grace."

I hear applause and 'amen' from many in the congregation. Someone is walking up the middle aisle to give their life to Christ. I clap even though I can't see who it is for the podium in front of me. Pastor Collins speaks loudly into the microphone.

"Look at God. Don't we serve a mighty God? He is forgiving. He is merciful and He is here."

He steps from the pulpit to meet the person in front of the podium. The other minister in the pulpit and I stand. Pastor has someone wrapped in a full embrace. He releases them. Angela. My heart leaps for joy. God is good. Angela told me her mother had her baptized when she was six. Since then, she has not had a desire to build a relationship with God. Look at her now. Her face is wet with tears. Our eyes lock. My smile is genuine. My joy is sincere. After our conversation at the restaurant, I prayed for God to heal both of us. I believe all she told me and believe she truly regrets her mistakes.

Pastor leans over and talks to her. He looks out and addresses the congregation.

"Sister Reynolds has expressed her desire to renew her relationship with God. She desires to be rebaptized and I am more than happy to help her with her renewal. It's not a matter of whether it is necessary to rebaptize or not, but a matter of one having what they need to be committed to God. Sister Angela, I am so proud of you. Know that your church family is here to assist you in any way you need. Come on down preach-brethren and sister and let us pray strength over our sister in the Lord."

The men in the Pulpit allow me to come down first. I walk up and give Angela a full embrace.

"Angela, I am so proud of you."

She breaks down into full sobs. I have to brace myself to keep both of us from falling to the floor.

"I'm so sorry Michelle. You were so good to me and I made a mess of everything. Please forgive me."

She sobs into my neck.

"Angela that is behind us. I forgive you and I love you."

She holds me tighter and her sobs become harder. I pat her on the back to help calm her down.

"Angela," I call her name to calm her down. Pulling her away from me to look her in the eyes, I call her again.

"Angela." She looks at me with a wet face. Someone hands her some napkins. "Angela, God has forgiven you and I have forgiven you. Now I am going to be there to help you forgive yourself. I do love you."

"I love you too, Michelle." She throws her arms back over my shoulder and pulls me into another hug. "You did so good and I am so proud of you too."

The other ministers embrace Angela and give her words of encouragement. Pastor Collins looks at me with that warm smile that makes me want to rest in his arms.

"Minister Michelle, will you lead us in prayer with Sister Angela?"

"I will be happy to." I take the microphone and we all bow our heads. The church stands with us.

After the prayer, all the ministers walk back to the pulpit and we take our seats. Pastor Collins stands at the podium.

"Come here, minister."

He turns and looks at me. As I stand, he reaches under the podium and pulls out a plaque. He throws an arm over my shoulder and pulls me to him.

Smiling down at me he says, "I don't know of anyone more deserving of this."

With his arm still around my shoulder, he reads the contents of the plaque. At the end he says,

"I Pastor Marc Collins, present you, Minister Michelle Hill with this license to preach the gospel. Preach in season and preach out of season. Preach wherever you go and anywhere you're called. I am so proud of you. Congratulations and welcome to the ministry."

He turns me to face the audience. They all stand on their feet. The room fills with cheers and applause. One of the ushers takes our picture. I return to my seat feeling overwhelmed. Pastor Collins, still excited, turns back to the microphone.

"After that, I have nothing else to say. God has spoken. I would like to extend an invitation to Dr. Philmont if he wishes to have a few words."

Pastor looks to the front row of district leaders. All the men on the front row look to the man on end. He stands and walks to the pulpit. Dr. Philmont is a very distinguished gentleman exquisitely dressed. He appears to be in his seventies, but well preserved. He walks past the extended microphone in Pastor Collins hand and steps in front of me. I look up at him. My heart rate increases. He smiles and extends his hand to me. I relax and take his hand. He pulls me to my feet and embraces me.

"That was impressive young lady. Congratulations and welcome aboard."

He turns and takes the microphone from Pastor Collin's and gives him a pat on the back.

"How have you been my friend?"

Pastor Collins takes his seat beside me. He looks at me with an approving smile. Dr. Philmont steps to the podium.

"All praise and honor go to God. Thank you, Pastor Collins, for the opportunity. I must admit, I came here skeptical. A female preacher is not something I wanted to accept. I have always believed leading is for the men only. Well, I had a member recently come to me and say she has been called into the ministry. I really admire this woman and don't want to lose her. She is invaluable to the church. I told her to let me pray about it. When Reverend Jones came and told us Pastor Collins was allowing a woman in the pulpit, I had mixed emotions. I needed to see for myself. God has been working on me. I came here looking for confirmation or a conclusion to the matter.

"I am glad I came. If that was not God, I don't know what is. Young lady, you have impressed me, and I don't impress easily. God is using you and I pray you allow Him to continue. God has a way of sending the answers we seek. Others may not be as receptive, but as for me, I'm a believer. God can do what He wants, when He wants and through whomever He chooses. Good job Minister."

He looks at me with a smile and approving nod. Then he returns the mic and steps down from the pulpit. Reverend Jones lowers his head and walks out the side door. I guess he can't accept the fact that a woman preacher is at his home church. The church is applauding Dr. Philmont and they don't seem to notice him leave. Pastor Collins stands to the podium and lifts both hands for the church to stand for dismissal.

After greetings from my church family and friends, I enjoy lunch with my parents. I go home overwhelmed and happy. God has really shown Himself mighty today.

Now, if I can just get this dinner, I must prepare for Pastor Collins to go as smoothly. I will focus on that next week. Today, I want to bask in the glory of my God.

"Thank you, Jesus."

Chapter 17

Being Mrs. Marc Collins is amazing. He treats me as his queen; as an equal. We talk about everything. He wants to know how I feel, what agitates me, what makes me happy and what makes me sad. His primary goal in our marriage is to make me happy. I find myself eager to get home every day just to see him. Each time I attempt to do something to please him, he finds a way to make it about me. He once told me that he could never express his love and appreciation for me, so he would have to show me. I knew there were good men out there but never thought I would find one. God is good.

We've been married for three months. I come home from one of those exhausting days at work. One where I would have called in a personal day if I had known what was awaiting me. Mr. Qamar was on one of his rampages. He had me running all over the place. My step tracker count is over twenty-one thousand steps. My feet are killing me. My normal goal is ten thousand steps a day.

I plan to cook something quick for supper. Marc's car is in the garage when I get home. I usually beat him home. I hope everything is alright. I rush in to see him. I'm met at the door by his warm smile and embrace. It feels good to be in his arms.

"How was your day?" he asks.

I give him a quick peck on the lips, exhale and walk to the couch. I lay my purse on the end table and flop on the couch. He notices I am exhausted. He sits on the couch with me, pulls my pumps off and put my feet onto his lap. His foot massages are remarkable. I lay my head back on the pillow.

"Ahhhh. That feels good. My feet are killing me."

"That bad huh?" he replies.

"I have been running all day. My boss had another one of his conniptions. He wanted first-hand description to justify his decision not to back the latest investment. Of course, that first-hand description was mine. I had to walk all the way out back to the testing center and watch as they tried this new product, three times. When I returned and compiled the data, he sent me back again to look at it from a different angel. Qamar was convinced it was not a good investment." I smile. "And he turned out to be right. The thing broke on my third trip. Smoke went everywhere. I was glad. I didn't have to make another trip out there. When I sent him my final report, he walked out of his office with his chest in the air, 'I knew I was right. If that thing can't make it through four hours of testing in the plant, how long will it last with our customers'," I said mocking Qamar.

Marc smiles at my animated description of my day.

"This is amusing to you?" I ask.

"You're cute when you're flustered."

I don't care what I look like as long as he continues to rub my feet.

I rest my head on the pillow again. Breathing in the delicious aroma in the house, I try to figure out what he is cooking. I could go to sleep. This is so relaxing. Until his hand goes up my leg to massage my calf. My muscles tighten. My legs are firm. I have been working out with him in his exercise room three times a week since we married. A vision of him shirtless and sweaty, on the chin up machine made my head pop up and give him that 'back to the feet' look.

He smiles. "You hungry?"

"I'm getting there." I never take my eyes from his.

He giggles at my attempt to flirt. He goes back to massaging my feet.

"I made your favorite. Lasagna," he says.

"What's the occasion?" I ask still relaxed. "Wait. Why are you home? Is everything all right?"

"Yes. I wanted to talk to you. I re-arranged my work and meetings to get home at noon today."

"Uh and, this talk requires you to fix my favorite?" I ask.

"Maybe I just wanted to feed you. You are getting skinny you know."

"I've only lost twenty pounds," I declare.

"Well that's twenty pounds less I have to hold," he says.

"My mind has not been on food lately," I smile at him. "And, throw in the way you torture me during workouts, the weight continues to fall off. I have tried for years to lose weight and all I had to do was marry a handsome pastor."

He smiles at me. "I just wanted to relax and talk to my wife today. What's wrong with that?"

"Lasagna." I say. "The only other time you made me lasagna was when you wanted me to go to your ex mother-in-law's house for one of the kids birthday party. You said you knew she and your ex would be there and you wanted to soften me up before you asked. I will gladly go anywhere with you. Your lasagna is delicious but not necessary."

"Well," he said. "I asked you this already and you said 'no'."

The foot massage intensifies. I lay back on the pillow and moaned. He can't possibly know how good that feels.

"So, you decide to cheat with lasagna and a foot massage?" I say. I sit up on the couch. "Hold on. What have I said 'no' to?"

I will do anything for this man. I can't imagine saying 'no' to anything he asks.

"Go change and we can talk about it over supper," he says.

He lays my feet on the floor, gives me a gentle kiss and heads to the kitchen.

I grab my shoes and rush to the bedroom. I yank off my business suit and toss it on the bed. I'll take care of that later. I grab some shorts and a blouse and rush to the bathrooms to freshen up. I hear dishes rattling from the kitchen. I hurry around the corner to a beautiful, candle lit table set with lasagna, salad and wine glasses containing sweet tea. I stop and smile. Marc is holding my seat out for me with his enormous smile. I step to the seat and pause facing him.

"Yes, to whatever it is you want," I say.

He giggles. "Be careful what you agree to. You don't know what I want yet."

That is true. I cannot remember what he asked that I would not agree to. He walks to his seat. Instead of sitting across from me as usual, he sits adjacent to me; within arm's reach. My heart begins racing. He still has that enthralling effect on me. He takes both my hands into his and blesses the food.

"Father, we thank you for the many blessings you have given us. I thank you for this amazing partner, helpmate and friend you have matched me with. Open our minds to communicate, connect and agree on the level you would have us to operate. Now bless this food for the nourishment of our bodies. In Jesus name we pray. Amen."

"Amen." I have a feeling there is more to that prayer, but I'll wait for his question.

"Let's eat," he says.

We eat several minutes in silence.

"Ummm. This is delicious." I look at him. He looks as if he's thinking. "Are you going to ask me what it is you want of me? It has to be big to have you looking so serious."

"Michelle. I love you."

"I love you too, Marc. More than anything. Please ask. If it's within my power, it's yours."

He runs his fork over a piece of meat on his plate. The last time I saw him this somber over something was the night he proposed to me. We had only been dating three months. Courtship with him was blissful. I always felt he was trying too hard, but he said a woman was to be treated as a queen and I deserved nothing less. He took me to so many fancy restaurants. I tried several dishes I had never even heard of. He said his mother is great cook and he became fascinated with food as a child. We went to live plays and musicals. He even once took me on a boat ride with a gospel concert on board. I don't even know how they did that, but it was wonderful.

He told me there was so much more he wanted to experience with me, but most places would require us to stay away overnight. He did not want to give people anything extra to gossip about. He was always a perfect gentleman. Our first kiss was on our wedding day. Although the day he proposed, I really wanted him to kiss me. When I said yes, he stood and pulled me into a full embrace and held me tightly.

I remember that day vividly. He took me to a fancy Italian restaurant. I still can't pronounce the name of it. He told me to dress nice, he was taking me somewhere special. I learned quickly his 'dress nicely' meant elegant. I wore my full length red, off the shoulder evening gown with matching diamond necklace and earrings. I bought the outfit for one of my office Christmas parties. I had only worn it once. I wore my hair up to show my neckline and a little more makeup than my normal. With some matching red four-inch heels, I was dressed to impress. When he came to pick me up, I saw his eyes light up as I opened my front door. He first took me to the theater where we watched a live rendition of 'The Green Mile.' I cried through most of the play.

Afterwards we went to the restaurant. He was wearing a black tailored tuxedo that made him look masculine and breathtaking. He stepped out of the car for the valet and walked to my door. He extended his hand to me and I stood almost brushing against him. My body tingled all over. He looked down then up my dress as I stood. Our eyes met and it took everything in me not to melt into his arms just to feel him next to me. I smiled and stepped away from the door. We had only been dating three months. Without saying, we both understood we were going to wait until after marriage to become intimate. When out with him, I purposefully chose outfits that were not too revealing. He is still just a man after all. That night, however, the gown I was wearing fit perfectly. It revealed more cleavage than I wanted, but I didn't want to go buy another dress when I had only worn that one once.

I was very comfortable around Mark, but the next step in our relationship was a big one. I had already convinced myself any kind of inappropriate behavior would have to wait. I'm glad he agreed and kept his hands to himself. Some days I don't know if I would have had the strength to resist him.

He took me by the hand and led me to the door. In the restaurant, he chose a secluded table in the corner. As usual, I look at pictures on the menu and watch him laugh as I try to pronounce some of the items.

His smile does something to me. I quickly learned to let him order for us. I love having him make the choice for me. So far, everything he has chosen has been exquisite.

When we finished our meal, he called for the check. As the waiter walked away, he took both my hands into his.

"You're quite an amazing woman. You take the blow of adultery and divorce and keep moving forward. I could tell you were in pain, but you didn't allow it to stop you from handling God's business and your own. I have seen separations put women down for months, and some never recover."

He looked into my eyes. His gaze was so soft and warm I thought he was about to kiss me. I wanted him to. He continued.

"Then God rewarded you with a call into the ministry. I was so proud of you. I know it may not seem like it now, but to be chosen by God from among the billions of people in this world is quite impressive. God sees deep inside us, much farther than man can ever see. Even I, with my limited vision, can see why He chose you. I love the Spirit God placed in you, but I see something else. I see a beautiful, smart, dedicated and loving woman."

I sat silent. He was opening his heart to me and I wanted to hear all he had to say. Without taking his eyes from mine, he went down on one knee and a huge diamond appeared from nowhere. Simultaneously, my breath stopped, eyes widen, and mouth opened. He continued.

"Being a good helpmate is not about giving a man what he wants but giving him what he needs. I don't just need a cook or someone to share my bed. I need someone to discuss my problems, listen when I'm trying to explain how I feel, tell me when my sermons are possibly offensive, correct me when I'm wrong, call me out when I say something crazy, hold me when I have a bad day, tell me when I hurt you and show me how to make you feel better."

He massaged my hands in his. My heartbeat doubled. I froze. Captivated by his words, I couldn't take my eyes away from his. He continued.

"I want to know what you think. How you feel. Where you want to go. What you want to do. I want to know everything about you. I want to be your helpmate as much as you are mine."

My whole body was mush by this time. It tingled from head to toe. I couldn't speak. Looking into his eyes, I knew he meant every word of it. He had endured as much heart ache as I had and we both wanted, we both needed to be loved. I wanted to jump into his arms. Please don't let this man kiss me. I will not be responsible for my actions. He held out my ring finger and looked into my eyes.

"Ms. Michelle Francesca Hill, will you make me the happiest man on this planet and do me the honor of becoming my wife?"

All the air went out of my lungs. Breathe Michelle. I stared into his eyes for a few seconds. Processing what was happening. I knew we were leading up to this. I hoped anyway. I have envisioned it several times. But to have it happening. Right here. Right now.

"Yes! Yes! Yes!"

He placed a huge ring on my finger, but I couldn't focus on it. I couldn't take my eyes away from his. He stood and wrapped those warm, strong arms around me. My body exploded with joy. The joy of happiness, of fulfilment, of being able to receive the love I wanted to give. Marc Collins is all the man I will ever need.

He held me in a long embrace. The restaurant is filled with applause and cheers.

"I love you," he whispered in my ear.

"And I love you."

***

How we went from the joys of marital bliss to a lasagna dinner and me trying to figure out what I said 'no' to is unclear to me. He is still holding my hands trying to ask something of me that I apparently declined him previously. I am eager to hear what it is. He continues his inquiry.

"Do you remember before we married, we compiled a list of question to ask each other to make sure everything was in the open before we married?"

"Yes, I remember that," I reply. A month before our wedding, he said we needed to get everything out in the open. He said he always suggested couples he officiated answer a questionnaire and sit down to discuss their answers before they married. He suggested He and I do the same and add anything else we wanted to discuss or ask to the list. He said nothing about a marriage should be assumed. Ask and discuss everything. And we did.

We discussed everything from living conditions, to bill paying, felonies, future plans, medical situations to credit scores. We even discussed sex although I wish we hadn't. That conversation put images in my head that made it hard to sleep for a few nights. I was nervous about asking for kids since his three are already grown up and out of house. But he gladly agreed to have more if I wanted, which I did. I can't remember any question from that conversation that I would not agree to. He looks at me and finally lets me know what he wants.

"I asked if you would be willing to quit your job and work with me full time in the ministry. You said you wanted to be able to pull your own weight in the marriage. I told you I had that covered."

"I remember that conversation. We discussed it. I didn't say a definite no. We agreed to give it time and see how things go."

The look in his eyes tells me it's time for him, but I am not ready to quit my job.

"Marc, I don't want to be a burden."

"Michelle, you will not be a burden. We have the money. I make enough to support both of us and then some. With my church salary and being a part time stockbroker, I can more than supply. And if the need ever arises, I will simply take on more clients. When I see you come home exhausted as you did today, I want to sweep you up in my arms and take you away from all of that."

"My job is not all bad. Most days are not as hectic as today."

"That's not the only reason'" he continues. "The district has our ten-day Annual Pastoral Convention in Florida next month and I want my wife there with me. Every year, I have to watch the other first ladies support their husbands and I am there alone."

"I can talk to Qamar and take the time off."

He rotates my hand in his and covers it with his other hand.

"It's not just that. I miss you and I want you with me during the day. That and you will be such a great asset to the ministry."

"That is part of the reason I don't want to quit work, Marc. I love the way I feel when I see you at the end of the day. There is a warm flush all over me. I have spent the whole day trying to concentrate on my work and not you. And then to come home; the way you look at me. I don't want that to end."

He brings my hands to his lips and look into my eyes. "That will never end."

"You say that now. But what about five years from now or ten?" I protest.

"I say that forever."

I feel my resolve melting away. My eyes lower to look at our hands. "What would I do every day?" I ask looking for an excuse to build on.

However, he is ready with the answer. He smiles. "You will be over the Youth Mentor Transition Ministry. We've been working with the state for over a year to get the grants and everything in place to work with youth under eighteen sentenced to juvenile detention. The state officials love our large Family Life Center, which contains everything from the swimming pool, basketball court and game room. We even have the classrooms for Bible teaching and training."

He becomes more animated when he talks about the youth.

"The Transition Program has already been approved. You can adjust the dynamics the way you like. A team is already in place to support you. The kids will be vetted before being released to us. We start them with one visit a week to the center and as they progress through the program, they can spend up to three days a week at the center, under the supervision of our team and a state officer, of course. They start with four-hour training and end up being able to spend eight hours a day there. Can you imagine the positive effect we can have on them? They receive tutoring, Bible lessons, game time and mentorship in a caring Christian atmosphere. Who better to lead that than you?"

His proposal sounds great. The opportunity to impact young lives is appealing to me. He can tell I'm considering his proposal. He continues.

"I will be around to support in anyway needed, but I don't have the time to take on the project full time. Once they are released from juvenile, they have been exposed to Christ and have a church home if they choose."

He has put much thought into this plan. The only glitch is me. I love Marc and I love working in the ministry. But this is a big decision. A life altering event. I have my reasons for not wanting to quit work, but I can't say no to those eyes. He continues to plead his case.

"I will be the Counselor on file to vet and counsel all the applicants until you finish your Ministerial Counseling Program at the college.

The only downside is, you will make much less money than you make now, but I told you, we don't have to worry about money.

"When we started looking into this program, my only worry was who I would get to lead it. I wanted this program in place, so I moved forward in prayer. I have been coordinating most of the work and making the decisions. With help from my staff, we finally got everything in place. However, I knew I would not have time to manage it effectively. Most of these kids have had it hard and this is their only opportunity to make a change in their lives.

"I remember the day in my office when God said, 'here is your helpmate.' My heart filled with joy. Then I realized I had my work cut out. I didn't know how to get you on board with all I had in store. Michelle, I need you. You and I are 'one' and I need my better half here with me."

"This sound like a great opportunity for me and the kids," I say.

"So, what's wrong? Why do you look as if I just took your favorite toy?"

"Mark, I love you."

"I love you too," he says. "More than you can ever realize."

I look down at my hands. He places his hand on my neck and lift my eyes to meet his.

"What's wrong?" he asks. Compassion is all over his face.

I know he won't understand what's troubling me and I'm not sure how to express it.

"I want to work in the ministry. I want to work with you. I want to spend every waking moment with you."

"But?" he asks trying to read my expression.

"But I don't want you to get tired of me. If I am here all the time, you will get tired of being around me."

I do not want to be in another marriage where my husband looks for places to go to get away from me. I know too many marriages which operate this way. I used to be in a marriage like that. I don't want to live that way again.

His voice goes up a little. "That's what has you worried?" He pulls my head to his and buries my lips with a long kiss. I respond to his touch. He stands pulling me closer to him. Each caress, each touch designed to show how much he loves me. My head is spinning, and I gasp to catch my breath. When he finally releases my lips, he looks deep into my eyes.

"Of all the things we deal with in this world, that is the one thing you will never have to worry about. Woman, I sleep you. I breathe you. I think you. I am you. In everything I do, you come up. I literally must pray to concentrate on my Bible reading, studies and sermons. I pray this will balance itself with time, but I can never get too much of you. When you spend as much time as I did in prayer for God to fix your marriage, you embrace His answer and never let go. You are my world and I want you with me always. Finish your meal, I want to show you something."

"I'm done," I tell him. As delicious as his lasagna is, I don't have an appetite anymore.

We clean the kitchen and put the leftovers away in silence. I see him cut his eyes at me several times and smile. I still have that caution look on my face. He takes my hand and leads me to the bedroom down the hall, the one closest to our bedroom. He pauses at the door and looks at me with a smile. I'm curious. It has been over a month since I went in this room. I only enter to dust it. This room has the least in it. The other rooms were the kids. We keep this one open for the occasional guest. We have not had guest since we married. It only contains a bed, dresser and nightstand. Maybe he is showing me I need to dust it.

He slowly opens the door looking at me while he opens it. My mouth flies open. I gasp for breath. A nursery? How could he know? I'm only a week late. My doctor's appointment is not until tomorrow. I only suspect I'm pregnant but wanted to be sure before I told him. My eyes scan the room in admiration. A beautiful hand-crafted baby bed with a matching crib. A rocker. A dresser and even a toy chest.

"Where did all this come from?" I ask still astonished.

"I made them," he says with an enormous smile. "My father was a furniture maker before he passed. I kept up the practice to remember him. It is just a hobby I do in my spare time."

"But how could you know?" I ask with awe.

"Know what? Wait, you're pregnant?" He pulls me into his arms and lifts me off the floor.

"Slow down," I tell him. "I'm late. My doctor's appointment is not until tomorrow. If you didn't know, why do all of this and when did you have time?"

He faces me and places his hand on my cheek. "I did this because I love you. I prayed for God to bless us with children and I believe He will. My part is easy after I prayed."

I see his eyebrows jump twice when he says this. "Yes, you are very good at your part," I tell him.

"I know you want kids and I want to have them with you. I started working on this shortly after our honeymoon. I kept everything in my work shop out back and brought them in a couple of weeks ago. I made these items for my other kids, but we gave them away when they grew out of them." He walks me around the room and point out the different projects he has worked on. "It has been inspiring working on them.

Thinking of my dad, you and us raising children together fills me with joy. Monday is my normal day off and I used much of that time to work on these. I wanted to surprise you. What do you think?"

My mind is blown. This man never seems to amaze me. I wrap my arm around his waist and press my head into his chest. I'm too overwhelmed for words.

"This room was always the baby's room. We wanted the baby closest to us. We can change it if you like. We can pick out paint for the room and paint the dresser, bed, crib and everything any color you like."

"It's perfect. I love it, and I love you," I tell him.

I couldn't say no to his request now even if I wanted to. I love this man and want to spend as much time with him as I possibly can.

"Can I at least give Mr. Qamar a month's notice to allow time to find and train my replacement?"

"You're going to quit work? Yes. Yes. I love you. Yes. Take as much time as you need, but not too much time." He pulls me tighter in his arms.

"You are my world and I am never letting you go. I love you Mrs. Michelle Collins."

His lips covered mine and this time he doesn't let me go.

A big part of my journey to becoming love is understanding I am loved. Jesus loves me. I know this to be true. But, so does Marc Collins. Help me Father to display and give the kind of love I receive.

Help me to *Become Love*.

The End

CPSIA information can be obtained
at www.ICGtesting.com
Printed in the USA
BVHW081111180920
589008BV00001B/110